WITHDRAWN

Quickies – 5
A Black Lace erotic short-story collection

Look out for our themed Wicked Words and Black Lace short-story collections:

Already Published: *Sex in the Office, Sex on Holiday, Sex in Uniform, Sex in the Kitchen, Sex on the Move, Sex and Music, Sex and Shopping, Sex in Public, Sex with Strangers*

Published August 07: *Love on the Darkside: A Collection of Paranormal Erotica* (short-stories and fantasies)

Quickies – 5

A Black Lace erotic short-story collection

BLACK LACE

Black Lace books contain sexual fantasies.
In real life, always practise safe sex.

This edition published in 2007 by
Black Lace
Thames Wharf Studios
Rainville Road
London W6 9HA

Academic Attraction	© Mandy M. Roth
Butter Fingers	© Maddie Mckeown
Doing a Number on Him	© Lisa Sedara
Ramraiders	© Nuala Deuel
Precipitous Passions	© Michelle M Pillow
The Apprentice	© Fiona Locke

A catalogue record for this book is available from the British Library.

www.black-lace-books.com

Typeset by SetSystems Limited, Saffron Walden, Essex

Printed in the UK by CPI Bookmarque, Croydon, CR0 4TD

ISBN 978 0 352 34130 3

Academic Attraction
Mandy M. Roth

'So, what do you think?'

Haley stared wide-eyed at Professor Gregory. The noonday sun filtered in the open screen door and caught the highlights of his blond hair, leaving her gaze tracing the edges of his stubble-covered jawline. She looked around the tiny lakeside cottage in the hope he wouldn't notice her lingering stare. The whitewashed antique furnishings and scattered lanterns lent to the nautical theme without taking away from the quaint Midwest cottage atmosphere. Sure, the majority of the shoreline of Lake Erie in Ohio was attractive but the tiny town of Marblehead seemed removed from the rest of the state. It was beautiful, so serene and secluded that it was easy to lose oneself. 'It's perfect! Thanks so much for suggesting this, Professor.'

'No problem, Haley. And I've told you before to call me Mike. I've always been adamant about that with all my students. I hardly picture myself as a professor, and it's not as though I'm teaching grade school.' He flashed a white smile.

Haley nodded and set her bags down on the hardwood floor. After placing her art box on the tiny table, she glanced out the window at the wooded area surrounding the cottage. 'It is nestled in so tight. I never realised something this beautiful was within driving range from the university. I can't believe how peaceful it is here. I haven't seen anyone since we arrived. I keep waiting for someone to show up and tell me the place is closed or that we're trespassing.'

'I told you that I know the owners,' Mike said with a chuckle. 'They set it up so I can come whenever I want during the off season without interruptions. There's nothing worse than having some summer tourist babbling non-stop when you're in the creative zone.'

Haley laughed and turned. 'Speaking of being in the "creative zone", when do you want to get started?' For a split second, she could have sworn that Mike's eyes darted towards the double bed against the back wall. No doubt she was letting her overactive imagination run wild.

'I thought we'd spend the day out on the pier. This time of day, you can see all the way across the bay to the lighthouse. It's spectacular, and knowing Canada is just beyond it adds to the charm. Depending on the weather, we might even take a boat ride to the other islands. It would be good to get some pastel time in there. It's too beautiful this time of day not to. I'm not sure how many boaters will be out. It's a bit early in the season for them. We can head back out there in the morning with watercolours. We might even get lucky and have some fog roll in.'

Haley beamed. 'That sounds great! So, should I meet you out there?' She bit her lower lip and glanced past Mike's shoulder, not sure where the pier actually was.

'I can wait for you. I mean, the last thing I want to

do is spend my spring break organising a search party for you,' he said with a slight laugh.

Haley rolled her eyes playfully and grabbed her art box. 'You just can't stop rubbing in how directionally challenged I am, can you? The entire class already thinks I'm flighty.'

'Well, you have to admit that you still get lost on campus and you're a senior now. Think about it, you've been my teaching assistant for over a year now and yet you still get all turned around in the art building.'

'Sometimes I'm too focused on other things to pay attention to where I'm going.'

He grinned. 'You should cut back on that before you walk into a door – *again!*'

Haley groaned. 'We're not bringing that up again, are we?'

Mike smiled and shifted. 'No, I'm willing to let that one go. But how many times have you done that so far?'

Haley's eyes darted to his groin. *He's my teacher, stop looking. He's my teacher.* She swallowed the lump in her throat when she saw the bulge beneath his faded jeans. 'I, um . . . I can't remember.'

'Short-term memory loss from cracking your head too many times,' he mused as he leaned forward to take her art box from her. His hand slid over hers and fire shot up her arm. His thumb rubbed past her wrist and the heat went to her cheeks. 'Are you ready?'

She looked him over, letting her gaze linger longer than it should over his groin again. *Yeah, I'm ready.* Haley nodded and followed Mike out the screen door. It creaked loudly as she walked out, and the wooden porch floor gave slightly under their combined weight. She glanced over and caught sight of something brown scurrying under the porch. She yelped and backed up.

Mike turned and followed her gaze. He cocked an eyebrow and the corners of his mouth pulled up. 'Afraid of chipmunks, are you? Hmm, I've always found them to be quite harmless, but to each his own.'

Haley gave him a droll look and laughed slightly. 'I thought it was a mouse.'

He winked at her and motioned towards a large willow tree across the way from them. It grew half in the grass and half in the sand leading down to the beach. Its large weeping branches hung almost to the ground. 'There's a great spot just beyond there.'

Her attention drew back to Mike's profile and she found herself nodding in agreement as she soaked him in. Haley followed him as he led her past the willow tree and down a narrow path. Various trees and shrubs lined the sides and Mike was quick to point out the blue jay darting in and out of their way. The path opened into a large grassy area on the end of what looked like a small peninsula. Rocks lined the edges of it. It was beautiful and felt so private even though they were in plain view of any boaters that may pass by.

Mike walked over to a large maple tree and pulled his art box and pads of paper out from behind it. He watched out of the corner of his eye as Haley took in the scenic view. He knew she'd love it. That's why he'd insisted they take a 'working holiday' together.

Having pulled a folded blanket from his bag, Mike turned and spread it out under the shade of the tree.

He sat down and leaned back on one elbow as he watched Haley peer over the edge at the water. When the slightest of breezes caught her long floral skirt, his heart slammed in his chest. It looked almost sheer on her with the spot the sun was in. The clear outline of her long legs and tight ass made his cock hard. What was he thinking bringing her here? Not work, that much was for sure. It's not like he made a habit of attempting to seduce students. But, something was different about her. Her very presence left him with an erection, and her sultry laugh had almost caused him to cream his jeans on numerous occasions.

This week away with her was wrong for so many reasons but he'd planned it all the same. The hopes of getting to sink himself deep within her outweighed the fear of the university officials finding out. Of course, if things went according to plan, he'd have her and keep it a secret too. No need to get the administration all worked up if he didn't have to. He had to admit that part of Haley's lure was how forbidden she was. From the moment she'd stepped into his classroom three years ago, he'd wanted her. The idea of having her rose-coloured lips wrapped around his cock while her blue eyes stared up at him had been the theme of many a workday fantasy.

He'd even taken to masturbating with the image of Haley spread beneath him, with her long chestnut hair fanned out on the bed and her legs wrapped tight around him. And the thought of her naked breasts being close enough to taste, touch, suck, he could hardly control himself. The last thing he wanted to do was sketch some damn lighthouse. No. Mike wanted to fuck the hell out of the little beauty next to him for the next week and then steal away after working hours and fuck her some more.

His body tightened to the point of pain when Haley pulled her sweater over her head. Her white blouse lifted, exposing her toned stomach to him. The thought of nibbling her ribcage on his way down to between her legs made him smile.

Haley glanced over and gave him a puzzled look. 'What's so funny? You're not still laughing at me being afraid of a chipmunk, are you?'

'So, you're admitting you were scared of it now, huh?'

Heat crept through her cheeks and he wanted desperately to see that happen while he fucked her. She approached the blanket slowly, her eyes fixed on him. As she sat down, her skirt got tucked beneath her and pulled high, exposing the rounded curve of one ass cheek.

Mike growled and wiped the palm of his hand across his pant leg. Every ounce of him wanted to slide his hand up her silky thigh and see if she was as tight as he thought she was. Before he knew it, his hand was on her, touching her smooth skin, feeling the heat of her body. Haley gasped. He took hold of her skirt and pulled it gently over her, covering her from his view. 'Sorry, your skirt was ... um ... tucked up a bit.'

She gave a small nod and pulled it all the way down. Now that he'd seen a view, he knew he'd have to have a taste, and soon. His penis jerked and dug painfully into his zipper. Relief couldn't wait. Quickly, Mike stood and forced a smile on to his face. 'I, erm

... I left something back at the cottage. Will you be OK out here for a little bit?'

Haley looked up sceptically at him and nodded. 'Sure. Will you be gone long?'

Judging from the size of his erection, it would take one hell of a thrapping to relieve the tension in it. 'Maybe, but I'll do my best to hurry.'

He walked down the path towards the cottages and waited until he was well hidden before stopping. From this vantage point, he could watch Haley draw as he relieved the tension in his penis. Unbuttoning his pants, he freed his erection. It bobbed obscenely before him and he grabbed hold of it. He wasn't gentle. Taking hold of his tight balls, he pulled any remaining loose skin back as he brought his other hand up. With a tiny bit of spit on his hand, Mike worked his dick once, twice, three times over before he found himself staring intently at Haley's back.

He built himself up to greater arousal, greater stiffness, massaging himself while watching her. She glanced nervously behind her several times. Knowing she couldn't see him as he stroked himself turned him on even more. Haley leaned back and closed her eyes. The sight of her resting was too perfect. The sun caught the highlights in her hair and she radiated beauty. When Haley shifted slightly on the blanket, her blouse opened, exposing a perfect set of perky breasts. Her nipples were darker than he'd have guessed and he couldn't wait to draw one into his mouth as he rode her. Mike could only imagine what it would be like to touch one, to hold one. Did Haley ever touch them? Did she ever play with herself? Did she ever think of him?

Mike grunted and jerked his hips as he focused on

her. His gaze never left her body as he tightened his grip, working himself harder, faster. Haley smiled lazily in his direction and, for a moment, he wondered if she could actually see him. Dismissing the thought as silly, he continued to pump himself until he felt the build up that led to the explosion.

He cried out, his mouth falling open as he hit his zenith. Come shot forth from him, hitting the tree in front of him. He used one hand to steady himself while yet more semen spurted out; he had certainly worked up a load.

When he had spent all his fluid, he tried to tuck himself back into his jeans but he was still too erect to fit comfortably. He needed to fuck Haley and soon. He couldn't go on with this endless self-pleasure. He wanted to see her face in the rapture of arousal – with him the cause of it. He was almost certain that she was as horny as he was, and he decided he'd step up the pace a bit.

He shuffled his feet and rustled a few branches to signify his return. Haley sat up and adjusted her blouse. Slowly pulling a sketch pad on to her lap, she looked off towards the lighthouse.

'How's it going?' he asked, his voice slightly strained from his massive exertions.

Haley smiled up at him. 'Mmm, it's great. I was just enjoying the view while you were gone.' Her gaze went directly to his groin before raking slowly up his body.

Nervous that she'd seen him, Mike glanced back towards the spot he'd chosen to hide in. When he saw the tree he'd stood behind in plain view, his heart hammered in his chest. He looked down at Haley, worried she'd not only think him a pervert but assume he was out to get inside her pants. While she would be right in assuming that, it didn't make the desire to take her appropriate.

'Sit down. You're missing out on some great light,' she said, smiling slightly. 'I absolutely love it here. There's no place I'd rather spend my break.'

He slid down next to her and grabbed a pad of paper. He stared at her profile, waiting for the right moment to say something to her. Had she seen him masturbating? Suddenly, the idea that she'd seen him stroking his cock excited him.

This is beyond wrong. Tell her to go. Leave yourself.

Haley turned and locked eyes with him. His concerns flooded away. It seemed as though the sounds of the lakeshore intensified tenfold while they stared at each other in silence. The water continued to make slapping sounds against the rocks at the base of the pier and the sound of birds chirping nearby reminded him of the blue jay they'd seen on the way out here.

Haley watched Mike as he slid his shoes on to go. After spending the afternoon sketching on the pier, they'd decided on setting up near the woods to draw for a bit. As it grew dark, they'd headed back to the cottages and ate. Haley was surprised to find that Mike was quite the cook. The pasta he'd made was divine. Watching him eat it was even better. Each time he took a bite, she'd imagined his lips over her sex. By the time they were done with their second bottle of wine, Haley's panties were moist and her body was in a state of need.

After dinner, they'd moved to the extra long lyre-shaped white sofa. Haley was shocked to find such an expensive piece in a lakeside cottage, but it worked well. Its scrolled arms and soft pillows welcomed her as she stretched out for a bit and, before she knew it, Mike was tickling her feet, which had somehow ended up on his lap. She pulled them away fast and he leaned forward to grab his own shoes.

'It's late and you're tired,' Mike said softly.

Haley nodded despite the fact that she desperately wanted him to stay. The thought of him sliding his lean body in and out of hers made her stomach flip over in excitement. She shifted awkwardly and glanced at him through partially closed lids and was silent as he walked towards the door. When she heard the screen door shut, she exhaled. The need to run after him was great but she held tight to her position. Begging her college professor to stay and fuck her, while erotic, was not acceptable student/teacher behaviour. He was her role model and the best instructor she'd ever had. Being attracted to him was an accident – although a very unfortunate one indeed.

After a few minutes, Haley stood slowly and pulled her blouse over her head. With ease, she worked her skirt off. She headed towards the bathroom, in hopes of soaking in the tub to relieve her sexual tension. When she opened the old wooden door, something scurried past her foot. She screamed and jumped backwards. A tiny grey mouse darted past her.

'Haley?'

The sound of Mike's voice brought her back from the edge of hysteria. Turning, she found him standing in the doorway. The feral look on his face reminded her that she was only in her undergarments. Much to her surprise, she made no effort to cover herself. She waited, sure that he'd back away, leaving her to masturbate yet again, before notifying the university that she was to be removed from his classes. When he took another step towards her, a wicked smiled covered her face.

'I can look around for the mouse, if you'd like,' Mike said, his eyes never leaving her.

Giving into her desires, Haley reached between her breasts and unhooked her silk bra. The cool cottage air made her nipples stand on end. She glanced up at him, hoping that she hadn't scared him away. The moment his hands went to his shirt, she smiled. When he too lifted his shirt over his head, exposing his tawny chest to her, she gasped. He was even more amazing than she thought he'd be. His body was toned, well defined. She had to pace herself to avoid running to him. This moment had played out a billion times in her head. Each scenario different, yet the outcome was always the same – the two of them naked and ready to fuck. He was off limits. Right? God, how she longed to be with him, to see if he was different from the men, or rather boys, she'd grown accustomed to. Mike was in his mid-thirties, sixteen years her senior to be exact. The very thought of the sexual tricks he'd learned over the years excited her.

He stared at her with hungry eyes. It was now or never. She'd taken that next step. She'd bared her luscious breasts to him and he'd be damned if he'd pass up the opportunity to have her. It was wrong, but his body didn't care. She stood stationary by the bathroom door. Her breasts were fully exposed to him and her tiny white silk panties barely covered the thatch of dark hair on her mound.

He took another step towards her, unfastening his jeans as he went. His cock needed little encouragement to be ready. It had been prepared for three years. Haley tipped her head and her long chestnut hair fell in waves over her shoulder. It slid over her breasts as he reached for her. Pulling her into his arms gently, he let a wolfish grin spread over his face.

When she didn't pull away, Mike drew her tight to him. Her soft curves pressed against his firm body felt so good, so right. His penis ached for relief and, currently, it wanted to find salvation only in her silken depths. Bending down, he brought her chin up to look into her blue eyes as he fondled one of her nipples. He squeezed it between his fingers gently and put his lips near her ear. She shivered and he couldn't help but chuckle. 'Mmm, forbidden fruit.'

'What?' she asked breathily.

Before she could protest, Mike dropped his mouth down on hers. His tongue found its way in and hers rose to greet it. Within seconds, they were touching, petting, tugging on one another – as though they'd never get enough. Haley bit at his lower lip and moaned when he grabbed her ass and squeezed it tight.

He rolled her nipple between his fingers and bent down even further. When her dark nipple came into focus, he slid his tongue out and over it. He eased off it and blew slightly, smiling as it reacted to him. Teasing her nipple, he licked it quickly and rubbed his lips over it softly. She moaned and her hands came to his hair, pulling his head tight against her chest. Mike drew her nipple into his mouth and growled. Sucking gently, he worked her other breast with his hand as he edged his body down more. He pulled off her nipple and it hardened even more. He smiled up at her. 'So ripe ... like berries for the picking.'

Haley ran her tiny hands over his cheeks. She cupped his face and stared down at him, her eyes full of lust as he went to his knees before her. Her brow furrowed. 'Mike?'

Tugging at her panties, he slid them down her thighs. The tuft of neatly trimmed dark curls that lay beneath smelled of sex and of Haley. He drew in a deep breath. His eyes fluttered. Licking the front of her hip, he continued to work her panties down her legs. He eased them off her and tossed them aside. Eyeing the prize, he feathered his fingers back up her smooth legs.

Parting her folds, he licked along the outer edges of her sex. Haley jerked slightly and he grabbed tight to her ass with his other hand to keep her steady. Kneading her ass cheek, Mike continued to let his tongue glide over the rim of her slit, lightly skimming her clit.

'Mike,' Haley panted as she clutched his head tighter. She swayed her hips, easing herself into his face.

He smiled into her as her juices oozed out of her sex. Lapping it up, he growled at how good she tasted. So sweet, like peaches and cream.

She moved faster, pressing herself against his lips. Varying the degree at which he sucked on her bud, Mike felt Haley's legs begin to quiver. Her orgasm moved over her rapidly and he eagerly relished the juice that trickled from her body.

'Mike ... please.' She pulled on his face.

Reluctantly, he gave into her and stood. The lure of

her mouth was too great and he clamped his over it, seeking her tongue, her permission to continue. She bit playfully at his mouth, skilfully dodging and receiving his tongue at all the right moments.

She encircled him with her hand. He wanted to throw her on the bed and ravish her but she broke their kiss and dropped to her knees before him. Reaching down, he touched her cheek lightly and she nipped at his fingers lightly. 'Honey, I need to be in you.'

'You'll be in my mouth.' She worked her hands into the front of his jeans and began to slide them down his hips. When his cock bobbed before her face, she laughed. 'Who'd have thought "the teach" was going commando?'

'No, Haley ... don't refer to me as that. Here, with you, it's just me ... just Mike. Don't remind me how wrong this is. Not now.'

Nodding, she met his gaze. Her blue eyes were hungry and he wanted to be the one to satisfy her. She moved his pants down a bit more. Wrapping her hand around his thick shaft, she smiled in delight, moaning her pleasure. Mike mirrored her noise as she ran her hand up and down the full length of him. She let her tongue flicker out and over the head of his cock before taking him fully into her mouth.

'Ahh ... easy, baby, easy ... Haley, you have to ... oh, that's it. Right there. Deep throat me, baby. Take me all the way down.'

He closed his eyes in ecstasy as she took him all the way in. When he felt her gag reflex kick in, Mike almost shot come down her throat.

'Oh, Lord, that feels so good.'

Haley continued to move over his shaft. Each time he hit the back of her throat, they moaned simultaneously. It was even better than he'd imagined, watching Haley on her knees sucking him off. His fingers were wrapped in her chestnut hair while her blue eyes stared up at him. Her hot mouth worked him to the brink of orgasm. Quickly, he pulled her off him. She protested but he didn't listen. He'd waited three years to have her and now that he had the opportunity, he wouldn't miss out on it.

Mike picked her up and carried her to the heavily carved walnut bed. Laying her down across the covers, he couldn't help but think her even more beautiful then. Her long hair fanned out on to the pale-blue comforter just as it had in his fantasies and his chest grew tight. She was so beautiful, so perfect, so willing to let him have his way with her.

'Mike,' she whispered.

Her sex called to him, the taste of it still fresh on his mind and tongue. Unable to control himself, he leaned forward to sample her again. Parting her velvety folds, he inserted a finger into her hot wet channel, bringing his lips to her swollen bud and drawing it gently into his mouth. The taste of her was divine. A meal he'd never grow tired of eating.

Haley bucked beneath him as he varied sucks and licks on her clitoris. She clawed at the bed and rode his face while he fingered her. So tight. So hot. So his. As she writhed under the weight of his caresses, she hit her summit. Still he didn't stop his onslaught. He lavished a series of long licks over her slit, making her wiggle more. Nectar oozed from her and he moistened his lips with her scent.

She tugged on the sides of his face and when he met her eyes, he saw the need in her face. 'Please, Mike.'

The knowledge that she desired him as well sent him flying. Sliding up and over her, he eased himself between her legs. He came to a rest above her, in a semi-push-up, the head of his penis positioned near her cleft.

She twisted slightly, causing the tip to enter her tight core. His arms tightened as he strained to keep from fully sheathing himself. He took a few calming breaths, wanting this to last and last. It took all of his resolve not to take her roughly, ravish her until he was sated. Well, as sated as he could ever be with this luscious young temptress. She was his addiction. No question about it. A very wrong addiction though. One that could ruin his career.

'Fuck me, Mike,' she begged.

Unable to resist her any longer, Mike did as she wished. He thrust himself deep within her until he was all the way to the hilt. He smiled; his little Haley was every bit as tight and wet as he'd imagined; maybe even more so.

Pulling almost all the way out, he locked gazes with her and smiled. She closed her eyes and he grabbed her chin lightly. 'No, I want you looking at me while we do it.'

A grin spread across her face and she ran her hand down the length of their bodies. His cock had a spasm when she wrapped her hand around it and he fought hard to control himself.

'If you hold me, I'll never last, and the thought of diving into your tight little pussy isn't helping my control any.'

She released him. He slammed into her, making her cry out and grab his arms. Mike pumped rapidly, causing the brass lantern light on the bedside table to wobble. Breaking it would be a shame, but stopping what he was doing would be much worse. Her channel gripped him and his penis bulged with the need for release. Afraid of coming too soon, Mike slowed his pace and began to make small swirling patterns with his hips. Haley responded by clawing his back.

'Right there, oh yes, Mike, there!' Her cheeks were now rosy and her lips swollen. She was so close, teetering on the edge of culmination. She wrapped her legs around him, allowing him deeper penetration. 'Ah, you're so big,' she purred. 'Too big, Mike.'

Mike rolled to the side, pulling Haley with him. Waves of silky long hair surrounded his face. Looking up through the chestnut veil, he saw her shocked look and chuckled.

'You could have warned me,' she said, her voice low, sultry.

'I didn't want to hurt you, baby. This way, you can control the pace and I can watch you fuck me. Besides, a gentleman always allows the lady to go first.'

Her brow furrowed. 'Hurt me? If that was hurting me then you have my full permission to hurt me any damn time you like.'

'Really?' A sly grin spread across his face and he made a mental note to hold her to that promise.

She straddled his waist and slid her body over his slick cock. Her eyes widened as her body did its best to accommodate his size. She'd had close contact with a number of penises, despite her tender years, but by far, Mike's was the most impressive.

He ran his large hands up her sides and cupped her breasts. Tweaking each nipple slightly, he sent slivers of pleasure running through her. 'Do you like that, baby? Do you like it when I squeeze your nipples?'

Haley rode him, rubbing herself against his lower abdomen and drawing in deep breaths as she took him fully with each stroke. Nodding, she leaned forward and captured his lips with hers. The new angle provided additional stimulation to her bud and her legs tightened. A tingling sensation emanated from her toes and she rode him harder and faster. She sucked hard on Mike's tongue. He let out a muffled cry beneath her as her core milked him with a fierceness she'd never experienced before.

Mike pulled at her hips, driving her down on to his erection even more. His body went rigid beneath hers and she had half a second to decide whether or not to stay on him.

Haley began to roll off him and he clutched tight to her hips, holding her in place as he came in jarring waves. Her eyes widened as she took every last drop of him deep within her body. She broke their kiss and moved to slide off him.

Mike's eyes widened. 'Tell me you don't regret it already, Haley. Please tell me that look is the one you wear after mind-blowing sex.'

She laughed. 'I most certainly do *not* regret it. I was just going to let you get some sleep.'

He shook his head slightly. 'You're joking, right? I'm not done with you. Hell, I may never be done with you.' He wrapped his arms around her and held her close to his chest.

She nuzzled her cheek against him and ran her

fingers through his chest hair. Eventually she eased herself off him and collapsed back on the bed. 'I need a shower,' she said.

Mike kissed the top of her head and ran his hand gently over her back. 'A shower can wait. We need to talk.'

She smiled down at him and waited for him to continue.

'You know that we have to keep this – *us* – a secret, right?'

Haley bit her lower lip and nodded. Running her hand over his collarbone she let out a soft laugh. 'I won't tell a soul about us. You have my word,' she said, kissing his chest.

'Mmm, now that we have that little discussion out of the way . . .' Mike flipped her on to her stomach and rose to his knees behind her. She tried to turn and look back at him. He caught her and positioned her face forward. A dark sea chest propped in the corner caught her eye. A large black iron anchor was propped next to it, keeping the nautical theme and making the moment all the more special. Mike's firm grasp brought Haley back to the moment. Pulling up, he brought her to her hands and knees. 'No. It's my turn to control the situation. I want you to take every bit of me, from every angle.'

'Mike?' Her eyes widened as he thrust a finger into her tight channel. Her vaginal muscles seized hold of it, and she didn't need him to tell her how wet she was. When she felt the tip of his penis probing her, she moaned. 'No more, Mike. Please, I can't do this. I need a break.'

'Mmm, you're a hell of a lot younger than me and if I'm ready to do it again, so are you.' He thrust himself into her with one long stroke. She yelled out and pushed back against him. 'That's it, baby. There you go. Yeah, take it all the way. You like that, don't you? You like my dick crammed in you.'

'Mike ... yes ... ah ... Mike.'

Easing his pace, he found a spot that stimulated him just right and made her moan. Haley arched her back and he ran his hand up it, coming to a stop at the base of her neck. He gripped her neck lightly and bent forward to kiss her back. He ran his other hand around to her cleft and she jerked slightly when he plucked her ripe bud. She tightened around him and he had to stop moving his hips to avoid finishing.

'Ohh ... Mike ... there, oh ... there.'

Mike rubbed her jewel again, in hopes of eliciting additional pleas for more from her. He caressed her sex gently, tenderly, while she began to rock her hips back, forcing him deeper into her. His sac slapped against her as he drove with full force. Haley's body shook and then he felt her orgasm ripping through her. Unable to stave off his own, he came with a start into her, soaking her with his essence. He lay still, sated, his body pressed on top of hers, his breaths coming in shallow pants for a few minutes.

Finally he withdrew and she turned to face him. She sat before him on the bed, her cheeks flushed from their love-making and her inner thighs glistening from their combined juices. It took everything in him not to ravish her again.

She cupped his face and pulled him to her. Spreading her legs wide, her gaze flickered downward. 'What do you say to spending the night fucking each other's brains out?'

He arched an eyebrow. 'The night, huh? There's

still a hell of a lot I want to do to that tight little body of yours. How about the rest of the week?'

'Even better, Professor.' Haley smiled and pulled his mouth close to hers. 'Besides, I really want good marks in your class.'

He slid himself over her and laughed softly. 'I'll have to think about that.'

'You could always go back into the bushes and *think* about it. Or, better yet, think about it behind the willow tree.'

Mike chuckled. 'You saw that, huh?'

Haley smiled. 'Yes, and I can't wait to touch myself again as you masturbate. I don't think the tree enjoyed the show nearly as much as I did.'

Mike eased himself over her and grabbed hold of his happy cock. 'Good to know.'

Butter Fingers
Maddie Mackeown

Pristine. That's how he liked it. That's how he wanted it to be. With everything in its correct place. Lowry looked around the room. Neat, tidy, minimalist. A subtle atmosphere of tasteful space. The cool colours and sleek lines shouted 'style' in dignified and powerful undertones, reflecting Lowry's private opinion of his own personal charisma.

He stepped, with feet swathed in supple leather, across a designer's dream of wood-block flooring to the huge expanse of window that overlooked the Thames below, flowing tonight in a soft grey glide that moved in muted persuasion on its way to the Houses of Parliament just beyond the bend.

He was standing at the centre of a power base and basking in that awareness. Well, maybe he was a tad off centre but close enough, surely, for some of it to rub off onto him. He ran elegant fingers through recently trimmed hair, which was just beginning to show distinguished grey streaks at the temples.

He could hear Eva in the kitchen preparing for his guests. She was quietly busy as she was in all things to which she applied herself. Efficiency personified. She would not let him down, that he knew. He listened attentively, trying to make out her manoeuvres, but all he could make out was the odd clatter, bang or scrape. Oh well, he always left it to her capability and did not interfere. What went on behind the closed doors he could but guess. It didn't particularly intrigue him. He had a vague impression of gleaming steel shrouded in a mist of steam. As long as the results were stunning as usual, then he was satisfied. Eva was mistress of her domain.

He turned at the swish of the kitchen door and watched her go over to the table. She minutely realigned the perfection of cutlery and candles around the fresh flower arrangement that she now placed on the shiny glass surface, an epicentre of the night's proceedings.

'Is everything going OK?'

'Of course.' She spoke in a low pitch, husky with intimate resonance. Lowry was aware that she knew he'd asked the unnecessary question simply to hear her voice.

She turned the vase to an angle of better advantage. Late evening sunlight filtered through glass panes in the ceiling, lending a shimmering brilliance to the ambience, which enhanced the creamy richness of each separate lily. The petals held spattered droplets of moisture that glistened. Lowry thought that the white lily was an odd choice of flower for a table decoration as they made him think of death and funerals. He had to admit that they were elegantly beautiful with a wonderfully exotic perfume. She always chose lilies, God knows why, and she always used five. He studied them and she studied him. But he knew better than to comment.

'Will you wear the apron?'

She touched the ties at her waist and thought for a few seconds. 'Mm, I'm not sure; haven't decided yet.'

He watched her face for some sign of perplexity but there was none. She remained as unruffled as usual. He would love to go closer, maybe wipe off a smudge of cream or strawberry juice, but there was none. Her skin was clean and dewy fresh. His nerves tingled as he imagined her sweat-smeared. She was unbelievably calm and collected. It was almost as if she had sneaked in a takeaway but he knew this was not the case. He wanted to approach and smooth a loose strand of hair back into place but its luxurious abundance was neatly clipped back. How did she do it? Such a profusion of wayward curls all held by a single clasp and not making a bid for freedom.

'I think I'll keep it on.' Her words cut through his reverie.

'Yes.' Lowry nodded. Then changed his mind as he remembered the plans for the evening. 'No, take it off. It'll give the right impression for these two.'

'OK.' She checked her watch. 'They should be here in about half an hour. Shall I get you a drink?'

'Yes. Please.'

He turned back to the scene outside, where a barge was passing in a miasma of muffled music. Some other type of pleasure was in progress beneath its canopy, something to do with dancing and celebration. Lowry could hear very little of it thanks to highly effective triple glazing and the ultra-soft hum of the air conditioning.

'Here you are.' Eva handed him a glass of iced mineral water shot with lemon.

'Thanks.'

She went to light the musk-scented candles while Lowry sat on the sofa that was nearest to him, sinking into soft grey leather. She took a place opposite, relaxed but not languid, perched on the edge, poised for immediate action if necessary. Her swishy skirt draped around her knees, flowing in raspberry ripples, the fragile, clingy fabric strangely at odds with her organisational precision. It was just the right touch, thought Lowry, suggestive of the softly feminine in service to the male.

'Well?' She raised an eyebrow in question. 'Tell me about these guests.'

He crossed one long leg over the other. 'Barristers. Both successful. One divorced, the other unattached and ambitious. Both, therefore, always ready to accept dinner invitations. Of course, they work alongside some highly respected women and I think might like the idea of an attractive ...' He was at a loss for the correct term.

'Waitress? Housekeeper?'

'Exactly.'

'Or maybe the au pair. That would make you a dad,' she teased.

He laughed. Eva smiled, a gentle change to an otherwise rather serious demeanour.

'Isn't there something you should be doing?' he said.

'No. Everything's under control.'

Of course it was. He held her gaze, hoping to find a sign of tension or worry or excitement in her face, but no. She appeared to be calm and untroubled. He lowered his eyes to the gentle rise and fall of her breasts as she breathed evenly. Her top was clingy but not overtly sexy. She was one of those women who managed to be alluring without having to try. Classy and sensual. She moved slightly and he was amused to see the outline of a nipple becoming erect. Yes! What was she thinking? he wondered. He almost wished that his guests were not about to disturb this moment.

And then they did. The buzzer sounded.

Eva turned to glance at the intercom then back to Lowry. 'Well, here we go.' Her lips parted slightly. Was that the suggestion of a blush? Maybe Madame La Chef was not quite as cool as the cucumber that she had diced earlier.

They both stood, each tuning in to the anticipation that sizzled silently between them. Then Eva turned to go back into the kitchen while Lowry crossed to the intercom.

'Hello?'

'Lowry, it's Blake,' came the disembodied voice.

'Blake! Come on up.' He pressed the door-release button. In fact it was Blake and Sebastian, arriving together. Lowry took a deep breath. Yes, here we go.

'Good to see you again, Lowry.' Three pairs of eyes surveyed all that lay before them. Introductions and niceties duly observed, the men had drifted to the window to look down upon their world. 'Lovely sunset.' Muttered agreement followed by a pause. 'Sebastian and I are eager to clinch the deal ASAP.'

'Gentlemen, let's get straight to the point. Might I suggest that we sign the papers straight away and then relax into the evening? What do you think?'

'Good idea.'

With contracts duly signed and deftly secreted into Lowry's briefcase, it seemed appropriate that the three men took a sofa each, as if mapping out their own territories.

Eva appeared centre stage with a tray of glasses and decanter.

The three pairs of eyes followed her every move. Lowry was momentarily mesmerised by the thin gold chain that now circled her ankle. She had removed her shoes and the toenails glowed with a polished redcurrant sheen that matched her top. His eyes crinkled at the edges as he smiled inwardly. She always did this, threw in a surprise for him, something off key.

'This is Eva, here to help me.'

'In the absence of your culinary skills, eh, Lowry? Good evening, Eva,' said Blake.

Sebastian greeted her and managed not to allow his eyes to travel over her body until she had turned away. A gentleman indeed. He will probably be the one to watch, thought Lowry.

He frowned. 'Eva, be careful. You've splashed drips on the tray. Wipe it, please.' The stopper slipped from her fingers and dropped to the floor with a small thud. She hastily retrieved it and disappeared back into the steamy world of 'kitchen'.

The conversation was genially challenging and flowed with the ease of whisky-lubricated tongues and the natural loquacity of all three men. There was the time-honoured rumble of undulating male voice as they analysed various aspects of the financial, commercial and sporting worlds.

The briefcase disappeared as Eva tidily removed it.

'It's nice and cool here. I was in chambers today. No air conditioning or none to speak of. Almost a sauna! Sweated buckets – and then went on to the gym. Sucker for punishment. Must be crazy.' Lowry smiled politely at Blake, appreciating the well-toned physique of his guest, and took a sip of his extremely diluted drink.

Sebastian's eyes had been slowly taking in all the aesthetic detail of their surroundings. 'Have you been here long, Lowry?'

'Oh, about eighteen months.'

'Nice place.'

That's not all you like the look of, thought Lowry. Eva had come from the kitchen with a salver of canapés, offering to Blake first. Lowry was amused. Was that a wink? But as Eva went to Sebastian her foot caught the edge of the sumptuous rug and a slip of crab and tomato landed on his thigh as the salver tilted mid-stumble.

Eva's cheeks flushed an almost match to the tomato. 'Excuse me, I'm so sorry.' She hurried to fetch a cloth. As she knelt before him and dabbed at Sebastian's thigh, it seemed that anger was not the prevalent emotion.

'Please, don't worry. Accidents happen. I hope you didn't twist your ankle or anything.'

Eva smiled her gratitude. 'No. I'm fine, thanks. Maybe I'll just leave these here,' she said, placing the salver on a small side table. She refilled the glasses, a mere drop into Lowry's, and escaped once again to the kitchen.

The sun had finally given up on the day, with blood-red streaks fading to salmon pink in the sky upriver. Lowry pressed a button and curtains slid smoothly to drape across the window, effectively shutting them away from the dusky world behind a barrier of peppermint-tinged voile. Another button and unobtrusive lighting glowed into luminescence at the room's perimeter with subtle invasions of the deepening shadows.

As the men took their places at the table, they moved into an area of fragrant candlelight, teasing the senses up a notch.

Lowry watched and bided his time. Voices were raised and laughter became louder.

'They don't accept blame, of course, but nonetheless agreed to ...'

Eyes followed Eva each time that she served or cleared.

'... even though the main witness was out of the country. Diabolical!'

Emerald green of watercress soup was matched by the blackcurrant of richly red wine.

'... used to have an MG, real sporty little model ...'

Fingers broke into softness through the crisp crust of recently baked rolls and creamy butter melted onto the warm freshness.

'... advised to buy shares in all things African or Olympian ...'

'... a field day for construction companies!'

The bed of rice was bright with yellow, red, orange and sprinkled speckles of leafy green.

'Eva, more wine please.' Then in a whisper that could be overheard: 'Will you take more care of my guests! You are being lax.'

The two men politely covered any embarrassment with complimentary remarks about succulence and taste, admiring the tenderness of the stuffed pheasant that had been soaked in a complex marinade.

Meanwhile, Eva refilled the glasses, gliding silently from man to man.

'So what is it exactly that you do, Lowry?' Sebastian asked.

Blake was taking a mouthful of rice when the bottle slipped in Eva's fingers and caught the rim of the tall-stemmed goblet. The glass tipped over with a small crash, spilling wine in a trickle, which seemed to catch the vivid sunset. All four watched it in silence until Blake overlaid his napkin and stemmed the flow. 'Everything under control. Nothing broken.' He laughed, putting the goblet to rights again. 'A little mishap, that's all. Nothing to worry about.'

'I beg to differ,' said Lowry, his face stern. He looked at Eva. 'Come here.'

She went across and stood before him. 'I'm sorry, Lowry.'

'I'm not amused. You have embarrassed me enough in front of my guests.' He threw his napkin onto the table.

Silence and stillness seeped through the room as each person knew that something was about to happen. A flicker of unease rippled between the two guests. Or was it excitement? They glanced at each other but kept their silence, intrigued. Nerves of expectation began to bubble.

The man and woman held each other's gaze and neither backed down.

'Are you going to punish me?' Her voice was huskily soft with a slight tremor. 'I didn't mean to be disrespectful to your guests.'

'Nevertheless, you were disrespectful.'

Blake opened his mouth to speak then changed his mind and shut it again.

Lowry slid his chair back a little from the table. 'You must take more care and I intend to see that you will remember this in future.' There he paused. Neither of them looked to the two men nor spoke to them. It was almost as if the guests were no longer there; as if the two of them were alone, locked in a byplay of their own.

Then she moved, taking a small step towards

Lowry. He took her wrist and pulled her across his knees. He did not need to be forceful; she was acquiescent, even willing.

It was obvious what was about to take place. Blake and Sebastian were shocked but didn't interfere. Their silence became a collusion that held them on the periphery. They were watchers, waiting for the inevitable moment when Lowry would pull up her skirt. Would he also pull down her knickers?

He did neither. He simply rested his hand in the small of her back and spanked her, hard enough for her to wriggle and gasp. Then he stopped abruptly with his hand left lying on the curve of her bottom. 'Gentlemen, do you think that I am being too lenient?'

They were instantly drawn further into this bizarre happening.

Blake shifted to make himself more comfortable but did not speak.

A pause followed that didn't last long but was filled to its brim with seething excitement. 'Maybe you should be a little more stern,' said Sebastian, catching his lower lip between his teeth.

Lowry smiled a private smile. Yes, they were hooked.

Without looking at the other two men, he slid his hand down her skirt then pulled it up, pinning it to her waist with his arm. He rested his hand on the strawberry-crush redness of her knickers, squeezing the plumpness gently. He was aware of a slight movement as Sebastian leaned forwards fractionally. He could feel the anticipation of his guests as they feasted their eyes.

The lightly scented air had suddenly become highly charged.

With deliberate slowness, Lowry began to pull down her knickers until they were halfway down her thighs, leaving the buttocks naked between the dual shocks of colour. The plumpness was firm and creamy, with a light garnish of pink finger marks. Lowry proceeded to spank her further. Eva began to squirm deliciously and then actually squealed, although it was a sound closer to delight than pain.

When he had finished, Lowry told her to get up. Eva slipped from his knees to stand before him. 'Hold up your skirt.' She did so, pulling it up to her waist and he felt two pairs of eyes searching greedily for a further glimpse. He was quick to pull up her knickers before they had a chance to see much, leaving them wanting more. 'Now maybe you will remember to take more care.' He slid his chair near to the table and continued eating.

'Yes, Lowry.' Eva turned and went back into the kitchen, rubbing her bottom as she went.

The two men were stunned. For a few moments they were speechless.

'Gentlemen, please, continue your meal,' said Lowry conversationally, as if the recent scenario was commonplace instead of extraordinary. He smiled a challenge at them.

Blake spluttered a short laugh. 'Ha! Well ... you certainly have a way with women!'

'Don't I just!'

Sebastian kept his silence. There were the sounds of cutlery, as each man carried on with his meal. Appetites had certainly been whetted.

Talk turned into falsely quotidian conversation as minds were elsewhere.

Lowry watched for reaction. He peered through the

glass top of the table, well aware that the other two men were extremely aroused but could do nothing about it. However surreptitious, any fumbling would be on full view through a glass darkly and so they remained horny but civilised. What a paradox! Well, gents, where do I take you from here?

He had promised his guests a bonus. What had they expected? he wondered: gambling, drugs, a blue movie? Maybe, but not Eva, a prize indeed, the cherry-topped icing on the cake.

He watched as they glanced around the room, unsure if the lights had dimmed or not. The atmosphere seemed to have become warmer, with softer lighting, red infused.

As Eva came to clear the plates he knew that each man was thinking of the pink-marked bottom. Was there a faintly accentuated wiggle to her walk? Eating suddenly became a serious business as the men concentrated on their meal.

Dessert arrived in the shape of baked Alaska, offering another paradoxical delight. The coolness of fruit and ice cream, trapped by the sudden heat of stiff white meringue.

Eat the message, gentlemen.

Eva hovered, ready to pour sweet dessert wine, very carefully, of course.

There was appreciative chat while the diners added a trickle of cream and hopefully awaited further mishap, which sadly did not happen.

Lowry allowed himself two mouthfuls before placing his spoon decisively onto his plate. 'This cream isn't fresh.'

There was silence as the men looked at him, spoons suspended mid-air. Then Blake spoke. 'No, I don't think there's anything wrong with it. Seems fine to me.' He gesticulated vaguely with his spoon.

'Actually, I agree with Lowry,' said Sebastian, also laying his spoon on the plate.

I knew you'd be the one to watch, thought Lowry.

Blake shifted in his seat. 'Well, now I think about it, maybe you're right.' He too put down his spoon.

Three pairs of eyes surveyed the woman beside them. She gently placed the bottle on the table and remained still.

Lowry allowed the tension to build a little then spoke. 'Fetch what I want, please.' They're practically drooling, he thought.

Eva disappeared briefly into the kitchen, to return moments later with a spatula in her hand. It was made of soft wood, quite small and very light.

She gave it to Lowry. He took it and patted it thoughtfully on his thigh. 'To chastise the cook with her own tool.' He raised an eyebrow in rhetorical question and looked at the men, pulling them into his game. 'Appropriate, don't you think?' They said nothing, did nothing.

He stood, pushing back his chair, then slowly slid his plate away to leave a space in front of him. He moved behind Eva and pulled up her skirt.

A thin sheen of sweat glistened on Blake's upper lip.

Sebastian remained cool.

She was calm, complacent. 'Pull down your knickers,' Lowry demanded. She pulled them down to her knees. Her nipples were erect beneath the clingy fabric and her lips parted as her breathing came faster.

Blake looked at the top of her thighs, seemingly mesmerised by her shaven mound and the butterfly that had landed there in the form of a tattoo. He wanted to touch it, Lowry knew. The wings were outspread as if hovering, poised, ready to take flight.

Sebastian's eyes ran over her exposed body and the tip of his tongue passed across his lips. I know what you want to do, thought Lowry.

'Bend over,' Lowry said. Eva bent over the table where he had cleared it. He took the spatula firmly in his hand and lifted it, letting it hover for a moment. Then the sound of slapping cut through the air as he began to chastise her.

After a few slaps, Eva began to moan but it was not a cry of pain. She reached out her arms and gripped the edges of the table. Her lips were parted and her face was flushed. The soft smacks continued then Lowry stopped and dropped the spatula onto the table.

He stepped close to her, his belly pressing against her bottom and his knee pushing between her thighs in a stance that said, 'I am her master.' He reached to take the clip from her hair, which tumbled like a mane around her face. He buried a hand in the unruly curls, gripping and pulling up her head. Dipping a finger into the melting ice cream, he slid it between her lips. The men watched, fascinated, as she licked the finger.

'I offer you the final dish of the night, gentlemen. Not quite whipped cream.' He smiled, his fingers beginning to slide along her pouting lips, her tongue flicking the tips.

He released her, feeling the fizz around the table

like bubbles in a champagne bottle about to explode. He stepped back, slipping his hand smoothly into his pocket.

There was no pretence that this was now anything but sexual. Lowry had given a clear message and the woman was obviously compliant. Blake was about to make a move.

At that moment, Lowry pressed 'Call' on the mobile in his pocket. A telephone rang. Eva stood, her skirt falling into place around her. Everyone was stilled.

After five rings Lowry went over to answer. 'Lowry here.' A pause. 'Hold the line please.' He replaced the receiver. 'Excuse me. This is a call I must take.' He walked over to a door. 'I'll be some minutes. Please, continue.' And he left them.

Closing the door, he pulled out the mobile and pressed 'End Call.' He turned back to the door which he opened fractionally. He heard Eva's soft voice but could not make out the words. Blake nodded and she lifted her skirt.

He saw Blake put his hands on her, pulling her towards him and touching the butterfly while reaching round to fondle her bottom.

Sebastian came up behind her and lifted her top to bare her breasts.

Lowry watched as the two pairs of hands felt her. Heat pulsed through his veins. His erection felt huge inside his trousers but he would wait. His staying power was tremendous.

Sebastian crouched and parted her buttocks, touching and tasting the delights that had lain hidden there. Lowry clenched his jaws.

They pushed her back to sit on the table. Sebastian pulled off her knickers and threw them onto the floor.

She lay back. They blocked his view momentarily. Then he could see Blake feeling between her thighs and sliding a finger between her legs. There was a sharp intake of breath. Lowry imagined the warm smoothness.

Eva wriggled against the groping finger, which soon became two. Her legs were lifted and held open. The butterfly fluttered enticingly as she moved against the thrusting fingers. Sebastian pressed his mouth to the butterfly and his tongue slid downwards. The fingers were withdrawn and they parted the lips for his greedy tongue.

Lowry's face was expressionless as he looked from beneath lowered lids. The men were hungry for the sight of her pink, spanked bottom. They lifted her from the table and bent her over.

Blake pulled her legs further apart to look at her. Sebastian stroked the pinkness as he undid his zip with his other hand and began to fondle himself. He glanced to the table and dipped his fingers into the butter, which was by now softened. Slowly, he spread some onto her bottom and began to rub it in, his hand smoothing firmly across the plumpness. Then he spread some on his own erection. His fingers slipped between her buttocks and slid easily into her.

The ice cream would have been cooler, thought Lowry, remembering the heat of her flesh as he had spanked her.

With trousers now undone, Blake stood, sliding her from the table and pulling her head towards him. He slipped his penis between her lips.

Her breasts hung free, swinging as they used her body.

Sebastian began to rub the tip of his penis across

the slippery skin of her bottom. No direct penetration, thought Lowry. Don't come inside her. That's for me. He would wait and take her alone.

He closed his eyes. He closed the door, resting his forehead against the frame.

Some time later, in the dimness, supple leather shoes trod carefully on the wooden flooring towards Eva's bedroom door.

Lowry listened but could hear nothing. He pushed gently and went in.

A flickering candle added a delicate perfume to the warm air. The room was awash with muted light from a solitary lamp, which threw a spread of soft-hued radiance across the body of the woman on the bed and enhanced the creamy richness of her skin. She lay on her front with her face turned away from him, the duvet kicked down to below her feet. She was naked apart from the strawberry-red knickers, which rested mid-thigh and accentuated the flushed skin above. She was relaxed, although not asleep, Lowry knew. Her hips were raised slightly on a pillow.

He leaned over her to touch the anklet, then traced a finger along the fading pink marks on her bottom. She trembled slightly and spread her knees wider, tilting her hips to meet his stroking finger. He caressed downwards in inexorable slowness, tantalis-ing, until he slid his finger into her vagina and felt the welcoming warm smoothness that gripped him delightfully. He imagined the butterfly, hidden from view, in readiness to take flight.

He sat on the edge of the bed and dipped into the dish that he held. Placing the flat of his hand on her bottom, he began to smear her skin with butter, now almost as fluid as oil. After a few strokes, she began to writhe in response. He bent his head so he could lick the marked flesh. She will have to shower later, he thought. Maybe I can help. Her hips rocked gently and she lifted her hands to squash the pillow beneath her head, snuggling her face into its depths.

He carried on, rhythmically massaging her plumpness. He held the dish above the candle to melt it further, then raised his fingers to drip warm oiliness along her spine. She moved against his hands as they moved downwards, unable to hold on to stillness. He smiled. Shifting, he knelt to straddle her body and proceeded to massage her back and shoulders. She reached down to place her hands on her bottom and held herself open for him. He dribbled the oil at the base of her spine in spattered droplets, waiting until they joined together and trickled tentatively between her buttocks. As the trickle reached her anus, she started to pant and lifted her hips, thrusting up in obvious demand. He ran a finger along the crevice and circled the anus before pushing deeply inside. She groaned into the pillow.

He could wait no longer. He wanted to force his penis into her.

He removed his finger and stood, already undoing the buttons of his shirt. He quickly stripped below the waist, allowing his penis to spring free at last. She was pulling down her knickers. He yanked them off her feet and knelt between her legs, which she opened wide for him. Lowering himself to her, he pressed his skin against hers, his penis pushing towards her raised hips and thrusting into her. There was a small cry.

They both lay still, feeling the moment.

Then he began to move slowly, burying his face in her hair and nibbling her neck. She turned her cheek towards him.

He had to know, even though it was like a punishment. 'Did they come inside you?'

'No.'

The surprise of relief rushed through him. He knew she told him the truth. 'Did they make you come?'

'Yes.'

He didn't like hearing it. 'Are you satisfied?'

'Yes, I'm satisfied. Especially now.'

A glow spread upwards from deep in his belly. His thrusting sped up. 'What next?'

Her voice drawled huskily. 'Mm. Musicians, I think, or maybe actors.' A small gasp escaped. 'Something . . . a little more . . . sensitive . . . moody . . . creative.'

He had a picture of himself hanging around stage doors ready to chat up the artistes: Excuse me, gents, would you like to do things to a woman while I watch? . . . Well, of course, darling! Is she gorgeous? . . . Oh, yes.

He couldn't hold off much longer. She whispered, 'Make me come again, Lowry.' Her hips were thrusting back in pace with him.

It was part of the game, to talk, delaying the moment until they could hold back no more. Think. Concentrate. Keep your mind off this glorious sensation.

. . . Maybe approach a woman. They had not tried that yet. But the thought of Eva with another woman only added to the present excitement.

Fortunately, she reached for his hand and squeezed it down between her legs, fumbling with his fingers until they felt the spot. He rubbed at her clitoris. It didn't take long. She was already panting hard. He put the fingers of his other hand near her mouth and she bit on his hand as she came. He sank his teeth into her shoulder and her head jerked back. The pain of teeth and the pleasure of rippling muscles as they gripped inside her, both at once, a double whammy, was reward enough for the evening's work.

He slid his hands to her breasts as he worked his body on her. He licked at her skin, tasting the sweetness of butter and the salt of sweat. Or was it blood?

'Come on, Lowry, fuck me hard!' she breathed. It was a signal. He could come. He cried out at the moment of climax. He had her. She was his, at least for this moment. He had been kept on the brink, simmering for so long. His orgasm seemed to go on and on and at its end he was slaked at last; replete.

Their breathing slowed to normal though it took some time. Numbers on the bedside clock flicked to a new hour.

'Do you want me to stay?'

'No. Not tonight. I have an early meeting at The House tomorrow.'

He shifted his weight and reluctantly rolled from her.

'Maybe a mega session on Sunday? Just you and me.'

His sated appetite was stirred again. He could not get enough of her.

He got up and quietly dressed. He noticed a small glimmer on the sheet by her feet. The clasp of the anklet must have come loose. She seemed to be breathing now in a regular sleep-rhythm. He touched at her ankle and pocketed the chain, then gently pulled up the duvet and blew out the candle. Lifting the curls from her neck he kissed the teeth marks. No blood.

Switching off the light, he left the room and left the apartment, to be swallowed by the darkness of the night, to make his way back home through the city.

Maddie Mackeown's short stories have appeared in numerous Wicked Words collections

Doing a Number on Him
Lisa Sedara

He rapped on my open office door before I could pick up the phone and pretend I was busy. 'Yes? What can I do for you?' I asked, glancing at my Concord La Scala gold and diamond watch like I had only a hectic few minutes to live.

'I've got some questions, Ms Demmings,' the kid responded, unfazed.

'Well...' I stalled, staring angrily at the phone, willing it to ring. No dice. I'd been ducking the auditors the entire three weeks that they'd been examining the company books for their year-end audit, but it looked like I was finally trapped. Hefty bank loans and limited stock capitalisation made their presence an unwelcome necessity; it had always ruffled my tail feathers that they could delve into any aspect of *my* company that they wanted to.

'Come in and have a seat,' I eventually responded, pouring syrup on to a full-bodied smile.

There were two ways of handling nosy number-crunchers: the hard way – brushing them off, making their job and the accounting records as difficult as possible, until they, hopefully, became too intimidated to question you or your actions; or the soft way – soaking them in so much sugary kindness and useless documentation that they, hopefully, jettisoned their objectivity as they rushed to get the job done on time. I knew; I'd worked for a public accounting firm 25 years before, before the long hours and short pay sent me in search of private-industry riches.

'My name's Malcolm,' the short, stocky, brown-haired bean-counter informed me, as he parked himself in one of the big, black leather chairs that stood guard before my big, black desk.

'I guess you guys are just about finished the audit now?' I asked, flashing a picket fence of white teeth dazzling enough to snow blind a Canadian.

Malcolm adjusted his out-of-style tie with one of his thick hands, gripped a pad of green seven-column and a mechanical pencil with the other. 'Yeah, we're just about done.'

'I used to work for one of the Big Five accounting firms, you know,' I said, attempting to lasso the square-jawed auditing foot soldier with our common bond, waste the only face-time he'd ever get with me on idle chit-chat as opposed to tough Q & A. 'An audit is never really quite done, though, is it, what with –'

'Anyway,' he interrupted, 'I know you're busy, so I'll get to my questions.'

'Yes, well, only too happy to help,' I said, glaring at the open door; there was never a busybody secretary when you needed one.

'I've got some questions about some of the income-statement accounts,' Malcolm intoned. 'First, the "Other Expenses" account. I noticed a lot of payments to consulting companies going through that account. One company in particular – T & S International. I looked at some of the invoices and all they said was "Management Consulting Services". What work did

T & S International actually do for your company, Ms Demmings?'

I fingered my Waterman Leman 18K fountain pen, leaned back in my executive chair and crossed my long, black-stockinged legs. 'Catherine,' I said, smiling. 'Those amounts are fairly small, aren't they – for your materiality level, I mean?'

He nodded his blocklike head, his clear, brown eyes unblinking as he glanced from my silk-sheathed legs to my pretty face. 'Yeah. None of the individual invoices is for more than ten grand – way below our single transaction audit materiality for a client with five-hundred million in sales – but they looked unusual, so I thought I'd ask. What'd T & S International do for you?'

I ran the slender, silver-ringed fingers of my right hand through my lustrous, black hair, twirled a shimmering strand around my forefinger as the soft, pink tip of my tongue peeked out from between my crimson lips and moistened them. The kid had a hell of a lot of nerve for someone half my age, and an accountant to boot. I'd run across his kind before, however, in my past life – lily-white untouchables with puritanical streaks wide enough to build a highway to heaven on; plain-looking guys and gals on self-righteous crusades to protect the fidelity of every number they audited; charmless innocents with no real-world business experience, in other words.

'I can't recall off the top of my head,' I replied. 'I'll have my secretary look it up and see that she faxes the appropriate documentation to your office.'

Like hell I would! Ten individual payments of less than ten thousand dollars to what no one but me knew was my own wholly owned shell company, which provided me with jet-set vacations, weren't enough to hold up a large-scale audit. Now, if those personal payments were put together with the other payments to the other subsidiaries of myself and long-dead relatives, then the whole crooked jigsaw puzzle might come together. And that could lead to a qualified audit opinion, possible de-listing, my probable termination. Not to mention nasty criminal charges and shareholder class-action lawsuits.

'I need to see some evidence of the work that these consultants performed, and I need a name, a phone number and an address – so I can get third-party confirmation,' Malcolm remarked, ignoring my response, making it all sound so damned easy.

I slammed my chair upright, my baby blues turning cold enough to pour Scotch over. 'Your firm collects a significant audit fee from my company each year,' I scolded. 'And I don't pay the partner you report to – Lyle – to waste my time with insignificant, immaterial questions.' I stared hard at the earnest, green-as-money auditor, like any more sass might cause me to bend him over my knee, give him some good, old-fashioned motherly advice.

He didn't flinch. 'I'll need the information I asked for – immediately – otherwise I'll be forced to document your lack of co-operation, and my concerns, in a management point, forward it to the partner-in-charge of the audit, Mr Warkentin, with a cc. to the board of directors. As duly appointed external auditors, we're entitled to full access to any and all records that we request.'

It was quite the sermon, and it made my delicate, manicured hands ball into rugged fists. It was time to implement the last-chance plan. I slowly stood up, swung around my desk and sauntered over to the door, my hips swaying like a fish-tailing Caddie. I closed the door, and then sashayed back over to an antique filing cabinet and pulled it open. 'Well, let me see what I can find for you,' I said huskily, with a smile warm enough to penetrate the darkest heart of any accounting zealot.

I plucked a folder marked 'Miscellaneous' out of the cabinet, and accidentally on purpose dropped it. Papers scattered all over the plush carpeting, forcing Malcolm off his chair and onto the floor, to gather up some of the meaningless pulp. I stood there and looked at his hard, round buttocks, as he squatted at my feet, and then I unlatched my short, black, leather skirt and let it fall to the floor. He heard the seductive plop and halted his paper chase, turned around on his heels and tentatively fingered my abandoned hip-wrap. His eyes wandered up my slim, stocking-clad legs, all the way up to my lacy, black panties and sheer, black garter.

'See anything you can use?' I murmured, unbuttoning my metallic-grey blouse, sliding it off my buff shoulders to reveal a black lacy bra that had its cups full trying to restrain my overlarge breasts. I'd attained the ripe age of 45 only two months earlier, but in my business – in any business where ethics are written in sand – it pays to take good care of yourself, and I had.

Malcolm watched as I unhooked my bra and shrugged my shoulders, forced the stretched-out tit-holder to join my skirt and my auditor on the floor. I cupped my heavy, creamy-white breasts, rolled my jutting, pink nipples between long, silver-tipped fingers and formed a scarlet 'O' with my pouty lips, my eye-lashes fluttering. I wouldn't be doing a girl–girl with Jenna Jameson any time soon, but judging by Malcolm's red face and partially unhinged jaw, my performance had definitely gotten some sort of rise out of him.

'What say we forget about the paperwork for a while?' I suggested, before reaching down and grabbing Malcolm's tie, pulling him to his feet, pressing my hot, soft-hard body against his and kissing him.

And after applying a heaping dose of snog to the stunned auditor's mouth, intoxicating him with the sweet scent of my body spray and the sensual warmth of my big tits and velvety lips, I broke contact with his gaping mouth. He tried to splutter a protest, but I placed a calming, controlling finger on his smeared lips. I pushed him back against the desk and dropped to my knees, unbuckled his belt and unfurled his fly in the time it took to cross a t, dot an i. Then I yanked his pants and shorts down in one fluid motion and proudly greeted the hard penis that sprang into my face, brushed my nose and swelled even further with anticipation as I breathed on it.

His aroused cock topped out at the five-inch mark – short and stocky like the rest of him. 'God, it's so big!' I enthused, looking up at him with admiring eyes. Come to mama, little man, I thought, you're playing by the house rules now. I wrapped my fingers around it and his body jerked, and then I began swirling my soft hand up and down his velvety pink length.

'Jesus!' he blurted, his body trembling.

I had the overwhelmed number disciple in the palm of my hand now, and I torqued up the sexual pressure, tugging on him faster and faster, testing his resolve, my scarlet lips mere millimetres away from the mushroomed head, my sure hand a blur.

'Ms Demmings – Catherine!' he wailed, warning me that he was about to bubble over with excitement, so enthused had he become with my sales pitch.

I released his cock, let it twitch in the hot wind of my breath for a moment, looking at it eye to pre-come-glazed eye. And after the spunk in his balls had settled down a bit, I opened my mouth and vacuumed him into my warm, wet mouth, consuming him.

'Yeah,' he groaned, giving tacit approval to my executive actions. His knuckles whitened on the edge of the desk as he looked down at me, and I expertly sucked him, my tongue running a slippery descent down his rock-hard shaft.

I mouthed more and more of him, scrubbing the sensitive underside with my tongue tip as I did so, revelling in my position of power and feeling myself moisten with every enhanced, enthusiastic gesture I made.

'Mmmm,' I moaned, sending oral vibrations coursing through Malcolm's overwrought body, hot, humid breath steaming out of my flared nostrils and against his crotch. I pulled back a bit, released half of his glistening length and then gobbled him up again.

I got a tried and true sucking rhythm going, bobbing my head up and down with my free hand tickling his balls. He gripped my shiny raven hair in his sweaty hands and grunted, and I gazed up at him from between his legs, my mouth full of his cock, my head full of triumph at the easy seduction I had perfected.

'Fuck almighty!' he called out, blaspheming into

the air-conditioned room, yanking my head into his body and desperately churning his hips, frantically pumping himself to oblivion. I wondered what was going through his mind; did he really think that he was the one in the powerful position? He'd probably imagined that he'd been the one to seduce me – the archetypal 'ice queen' older woman. If only he knew. Poor dumb sap. Then he threw his head back, bellowed like a beast and shot superheated spunk directly down my throat.

I grasped his quivering ass with my talons and milked that dick, my cheeks billowing in and out with the effort, my throat constricting around his spurting hood, drinking in his lusty load. And when he eventually squirted his last white dollop of surrender, I disgorged his cock and licked the remnants of his integrity off its softening tip. Then I smacked my slimy lips with the satisfaction at a deal gone down well, and asked, 'Any more questions, Mr Independent Auditor?'

A month or so after my oral exploration of Malcolm's character, he unexpectedly reappeared in my office doorway. The audit fieldwork was long since over, and the financial statements, with a clean, unqualified audit opinion, issued.

'Hello, Catherine,' he said, striding in, before taking a seat without being asked.

I studied his plain, placid face, his bright, brown eyes and his authoritative body language. 'I'm rather –'

'Busy?' he interrupted. 'Sure. But not too busy to hear a business proposition.' He crossed his stubby legs, folded his oversized hands in his lap. 'I know that you're defrauding this company of hundreds of thousands of dollars, Catherine – cutting cheques to companies you own for services never performed – in order to boost your take-home pay well beyond board-authorised limits.'

'Get the hell –'

'But I'm not going to report what I know to the various authorities ... provided you hire me as your new vice-president of finance.'

I threw my pen down in disgust and angrily folded my arms beneath my breasts. 'You little punk!' I sneered. 'I've spent twenty years building this company – my company – and I didn't get this far by being blackmailed by premature ejaculates like you! There's a camera in this office, child's play, and it's recording your extortion attempt, just like it recorded our off-the-books suck session last month, when you compromised your firm and your accounting designation by consorting with a client. Not to mention set yourself up for a conspiracy charge when you didn't report what you knew. Sorry, buddy boy, no deal.'

He didn't flinch. 'My work has seemed pretty boring since I got a taste of the real world of high finance right here in your office. I used to think that good business was squeaky-clean business, but you showed me the way, Catherine.'

My eyes narrowed to gun slits, fired darts at him, willing him to back down. We were both in a bind – the one I'd fashioned for myself and he'd discovered, and the one I'd entrapped him in – and that was fine, as long as no one tried to tighten the tourniquet.

'You've got plenty more to lose than I do,' he went on, putting the screws to me. 'I'm young and inexperienced; it's easy to suck a guy like me in. But you're old, I mean old-er and more experienced, with a company and personal reputation to protect.' He smiled a bland smile. 'So when do I start?'

My brass cupcake routine crumbled like the Enron empire as I realised he was right. 'Next Monday,' I said quietly, knowing when I was temporarily licked.

He shook his head, rubbed some salt in my gash. 'Not soon enough,' he said. 'My father's got a bit of money, Catherine, and, while he won't give any of it to me, he's always looking for a good investment. I told him about your company – not everything about the way you do business, of course – and he wants to invest. Provided that I'm in a position of authority to make sure things are done right.' He stood up and walked around my desk, pulled me out of my chair and planted a sloppy wet one bang on my startled pucker. 'And he and I both think I should start work here right away.'

As Malcolm brusquely pushed his tongue into my mouth, trapping my tongue, I consoled myself with the thought that the first rule of business is adaptation: embrace change or die. So, I wrapped my hands around the head of the newest member of my executive team and fought an erotic duel with his sticker. The kid wasn't the best-looking stud I'd ever fucked for business reasons, but he was still plenty good enough to bring a tear to a mature girl's pussy.

He told me to strip, and I unzipped my sapphire-blue Versace and let it puddle at my spike heels, as he calmly kicked off his shoes, pulled down his pants and shorts and let his hardened dick catch a breath of fresh air. The guy was as cocky as any young gun loaded with come could get, and his prick pointed directly at my puss, thick and throbbing. I awaited further instructions, willing to let him run the show – for now, anyway. 'Let me see those big jugs of yours,' he said tersely.

'Of course.' I unhooked my satiny blue bra and let my boobs tumble forth, hang huge and heavy, riding up and down on my chest as I breathed.

He grabbed my tits and roughly fondled the hot, firm tingling flesh. My mouth broke open and I moaned; his hands were feeling so very good on my ultra-sensitive globes and there was a certain new confidence to his manner. I moaned again when the jacked-up exec bent his head down and started licking at my nipples. I gripped his square shoulders and watched as he swirled his thick, wet tongue all over my flushed buds, before inhaling one into his mouth and pulling on it.

'Yes!' I hissed, my head swimming, my body electrified, making the best of a bad, bad situation.

Malcolm spat my glistening left nipple out of his mouth and swallowed up my other, sucking urgently on it. Then my blackmailer shoved my boobs together and bounced his head back and forth between my nips – tonguing, sucking, slobbering all over them until he topped off his tremendous tit-play by jamming my mounds so close together that he could tongue-slap both engorged nipples at once, which he did repeatedly.

'I've always liked older women,' my younger-by-half business associate confided, pushing my right breast up so that I could lick my own slick nipple. 'They can teach me so much.' He rammed his tongue onto my tongue, excitedly helping me to lap at my rigid nipple.

'Fuck me,' I ordered, when I could bear no more of

his frustrating tit-play. The upstart never had the decency to try and find my sweet spot down below, or ask what I might want out of the situation, so the least he could do was give me his cock. I was aching for it between my legs, and my panties were soaking with excitement at his rough handling.

He unhanded my overstimulated boobs, led me to the front of my desk, and then spun me around and bent me over the top of its gleaming, ebony surface. He fumbled with the straps on my garter, then tugged my dainty, cornflower-blue panties down my *noir*-stockinged legs. I lifted my heels out of my damp underwear and spread my legs, anxious now to culminate our merger. I'd deal with the ramifications of our unholy alliance later – when I'd orgasmed a time or two.

Malcolm stroked the luxurious silk that covered my lithe legs, then abruptly grabbed my bare ass with one hand and ramrodded his cock into my sopping pussy with the other.

'Yes!' I shrieked, not giving a damn if my entire staff piled into the office to find out just what sort of transaction was going on.

Malcolm's dick dived deep into my greasy sex till he was balls-to-the-walls. Then he started pumping his hips, fucking my sodden snatch faster and faster, spanking my big, pliable butt cheeks with his hard-thrusting body as my damp hands squeaked back and forth on the high-polish desktop.

He sawed in and out for a good, long time. He was certainly getting his fill of high-class executive bitch and he seemed determined to have the upper hand this time around. He was loving the way our roles had reversed, with him the commander and me the subordinate. He grabbed me by the back of the neck and pumped himself to a frenzy, till he finally leaned over on top of me, grabbed my tits and hissed in my ear, 'I'm gonna fuck you up the ass.'

I didn't utter a word of protest – if we were going to work dirty, we might as well play dirty.

He eased out of me, polished himself with spit and pussy juice, and then pressed the bloated head of his cock against my butt hole. I quickly reached back and parted my cheeks. There was no point whimpering and playing the virgin. I went full throttle into slut mode, welcoming his unholy intrusion into my anus. I groaned, overcome with a heavy, languid heat as Malcolm's prick sank into my bum.

'Fuck my ass,' I whispered, 'fuck it.' I was dizzy with the wicked sensation of his cock buried to the hairline in my violated bottom.

He moved his hips, slowly at first, then more rapidly, sliding his meat back and forth in my chute, bum-fucking me with an assurance that belied his tender years. Then he draped his body over the top of mine again, scooped up and squeezed my breasts, tongued up and down my neck, banging away at my back door.

I reached between my trembling legs and desperately buffed my puffed-up clit, frantically polishing it as Malcolm pulled on my nipples, swirled his tongue around my ear, and littered the air with obscenities. The dirty bastard was having a party. It was no surprise to me that this seemingly decent professional employee was an animal underneath. Scratch the surface of any office-bound accountant in his smart suit, with his spreadsheets and forecasts, and a beast will spring out at the right trigger – the sight of a moist slit and a little slutting around. Underneath the pretence to civilisation they all want to get a smart woman bent over and fucked.

The violent slapping of his thighs against my rippling butt cheeks grew more and more frenzied, until he jerked up and bellowed, 'I'm coming!' and blasted sizzling semen deep into my stretched-out anus.

I rubbed myself like a woman possessed, and a mammoth orgasm exploded at the thought of his raw lust finding its fruition. My climax thundered through my quivering body, and the contracting heat of my cunt spasmed and throbbed until I collapsed on top of the desk, exhausted and exhilarated. Malcolm collapsed on top of me; my pact with the devil had been signed in white-hot come.

Malcolm continued to fuck me up the ass, both literally and figuratively, and it wasn't long before he and his father had virtually taken over my company. He installed himself and his dad on the board of directors, and put an end to my double-dipping in the company till. He used his father's money to pay back the money I'd taken, giving me 'a clean and honest start forwards', as he kindly put it.

I put up with the reduced authority and salary and perquisites, playing the part of the reformed, repentant capitalist cheat, while I secretly worked on some strategic plans of my own. And, when I walked into Malcolm's office late one night and caught him pecker-deep in the accounts receivable manager, I decided it was high time to take care of some unfinished business – old management school-style.

'I've got a surprise for you, Malcolm,' I informed him soon after his bad debts diddling, strutting into

his office in one of my sluttiest ball-breaking outfits –
a red, latex skirt and black, see-through top. My legs
were clothed in their usual night-shaded colour, and I
had a pair of silver-tipped stilettos strapped to my
feet. My push-up bra had me spilling personality, but
I wanted to make sure that young Malcolm realised
just what he was going to be missing – and just how
low-down dirty the pussy-eat-dog business world can
really get.

'Not interested,' he stated dismissively from behind
his desk. 'I've got real work to do.'

'Not interested in meeting my new husband?' I
pouted.

Malcolm's father ambled into the office. 'Hello,
son!' he hollered, snaking a stubby, covetous arm
around my narrow waist. 'What do ya think of your
new stepmom? We got married last night in Vegas.
Surprised?'

I kissed the morbidly obese, sixty-year-old type-one
diabetic on the cheek. 'We're all one big, happy family
now – at home and the office,' I cooed, savouring the
stunned, defeated look on Malcolm's mug. To tell his
father about my transgressions would force me to lift
the rug on his own sleazy dealings, and that would
make sugar Daddy very, very angry.

A smile of triumph graced my full-bodied lips.
Malcolm gave me a cold, sour stare, as his father
proudly eyed my voluptuous body like it was a trophy
he'd just won at the crap tables. It was going to be just
peachy living a life of pampered leisure for a change,
while my stymied stepson and unhealthy hubby labou-
red to keep the family business humming. And, if
anything should happen to my mate, well, I was more
than willing to pick up his controlling interest and take

over; I'd had a bit of experience running the company, after all.

Lisa Sedara's story, *Doing a Number on Him*, appears in the short story collection *Sex in the Office*.

Ramraiders Nuala Deuel

Soft, round, nut-coloured buttocks, lightly oiled and presented as though they were a dish waiting to be eaten ... A pale-pink cock, fully nine inches long, as thick as a handrail, wrapped with nubbly blue veins that would ripple and rub against the tight hole readying itself to take all that meat in. A relatively tiny fist enclosing it, that of a petite woman, the glisten of painted lips parting to accept the impossibly large head. Large, unaugmented breasts on a skinny ribcage. Suki liked that. She liked the paradox. Plenty and paucity. Little women with big tits. That worked for her.

She reached out and traced a fingertip along their contour. The woman's expression didn't change from its cast of confused rapture. She looked, to Suki, as though she were concentrating on the sensations ripping through her body, focusing on her approaching orgasm. Suki rubbed her nipples, satisfyingly dark and erect against the white bounty. She would cup those beauties in her hands as she fucked her from behind, enjoying the way they jiggled and spread against her palms, as if they might spill over the edge at any moment. She imagined how her tight, shaven pussy would look as she parted it with a strap-on. The previous page had shown her with her legs wide apart, her arms interlaced across her torso (which helped to lift and separate her breasts between them), her fingers teasing her lips apart to show her deli-quescent honeypot. Suki didn't care if she'd lubed up before the shoot. She could pretend all that juice was from her horny core. And Suki could pretend that she was the reason it was there.

She was thinking about getting her knickers off for a lazy wank when the buzzer went. She quickly rolled up her copy of *The Damp Patch* and stuffed it into her holdall next to the untouched sandwich box and flask of hot chocolate. This was unusual, being disturbed during her shift. Suki pretty much ruled the roost in the empty warehouse from 8 p.m. till 6 a.m., when Malc took over, and a couple of diffident cleaners, who she never spoke to beyond 'hi' and 'goodbye', ran their mops over the floor in a desultory fashion. She patted down her tight navy-blue uniform as she made her way towards the entryphone. In the cavernous warehouse – that was rented by a European film studio to store props, costumes and timber for set construction – the angry swipe of her thighs rubbing together as she marched echoed like thwacks from a headmaster's cane.

'This is Ace Crime Prevention,' she said into the receiver. 'There is nobody from Cups and Cuffs Studios on site. If you leave me your name I'll –'

'Suki? Is that you? Suki Wilde?' Something about the voice was familiar to her, but she couldn't place it. The video screen showed four figures heaped in shadow: three men and one woman. All were dressed in long leather jackets. The man speaking into the grille also wore large mirror shades and a beanie. In one hand was a digital video camera, in the other a briefcase.

'Yes,' Suki said. 'Who are you?'

'My name's Hector Furst. I'm a film director. I'm big pals with Johnny Locke, your boss.'

Johnny Locke. The man with the little yellow chicken shapes on his tie and a rubber ring on his executive chair, who had been stroking her CV when she went into his office for an interview. Had stroked it for the next twenty minutes while he stared at her breasts and informed her she'd be getting five quid an hour, like it or bike it.

'So what? You want me to turn a few cartwheels?'

'I'd like you to open the door. Didn't Johnny tell you I was in town today? That I would be using the warehouse?'

'Using it for what?'

Furst held up the camera and waggled it at the CCTV. 'Fil-ming,' he said slowly, as if explaining to a child.

'Nobody at Cups and Cuffs said anything about –'

'I'm doing a *film* for Cups and Cuffs. And us chewing the *fat* about it is costing *money*. Do you want to let me in or do you want to carry on tickling my tits about it? Because when Johnny comes down here later and finds –'

'Mr Locke's coming here? Tonight?'

'Around midnight, yes.'

'OK, OK.' Suki chewed her lip. She knew that Cups and Cuffs made the kind of film that you did not take your five-year-old nephew to see on a Saturday morning. She was simultaneously appalled and excited. She sighed and slid back the bolts on the warehouse door. She turned the latch and Furst came barging in, looking around him at the space, already checking the light with a meter and barking orders to the three people following him. She took a brief look outside in case Johnny Locke was already here and watching to see how she was coping with this situation – maybe it was some kind of test of her security skills – before closing and locking the door again.

Furst had his cap and jacket off and was assessing positions to place a tripod. 'What do you think, Saffy? Do you think we'd get good light if we nailed one here?'

'Whatever, Heck,' said the woman, Saffy, he was addressing. 'You're the man. I go where you go.'

'OK.' He started clicking his fingers. His mirror shades remained in place. He was dressed immaculately in a blue suit with a faint charcoal pinstripe, a pink shirt and a grey tie with a shiny abstract pattern, as if he'd let a slug crawl all over it. 'Neil and Guy. Get into your gear. I want to be ready to go in five.'

'I think, maybe, I should call Johnny,' Suki said. 'Or someone at Cups and Cuffs. Just to make sure.'

'Make sure what?'

'That you're ... you know ... who you say you are.'

Saffy started laughing. Neil and Guy joined in. Furst regarded them fondly, indulgently. He held up his hand and they became silent.

'Look,' Furst said, 'I'm already behind schedule on this picture. It's low, low budget and what you see here is the staff. Director, producer, actors, cameraman, best boy, gaffer and bleeding key grip. We are *it*. If you keep fannying around like this, I'm going to be in the red so deep I'll look like Father fucking Christmas. Now you go and make us some tea, keep quiet for a couple of hours, and I'll make it worth your while. Shall we say, two hundred pounds?'

Suki clenched her jaw. Something about him was so familiar it was making her brain hurt. She must have seen him on the television. 'Two hundred pounds,' she said. That was the equivalent of ten shifts. 'I'll think about it.'

'Fine,' Furst said. 'But do it *quietly*.'

Suki went back to the little office where she spent most of her time. At the rear there was a kettle and a Tupperware box filled with teabags. While she waited for the water to boil, she wondered if what she was doing was right. But her mind kept sliding away from this moral dilemma. It kept wanting to focus on Saffy's soft red hair and criminally high cheekbones. It lingered on Guy's tight arse beneath his distressed blue Diesels. It was distracted by the swollen mass curling against Neil's left thigh. Why was it that she only ran into interesting, sexy people when she was wrapped up in her frumpy work gear? She wanted to storm back out there and shriek at them that she was sexy too. And interesting. And funny. And talented. Being a nightwatchman was just a way to keep the wolves from the door. She had plans. She had a future.

She poured water into cups. Caught sight of her face in the mirror. How tired she looked. How old. And she was what? Twenty-eight. She breathed in deeply. She could look good in front of a movie camera. She had great tits. Her ex-boyfriends had all drooled over them. Like juicy apples, one of them, Adam, had said. Firm and packed. Nipples up top. Always the sign of a great boob. Flat tummy. Succulent, greedy puss. An arse she could pick up pencils with, it was so tight. OK, so her face was a little plain. Her legs not so long. But she had more than most. She was blessed with plenty. She just wished more people would give her credit for that. An ordinary face ruined everything. She had a body that, at school, had made

everyone else look flabby or geeky or, at best, nonde-
script. But because she didn't have Tamara Bowden's
pouty lips, or Debra Houghton's shock-green eyes, or
Steph Moulton's slathers of caramel-brown hair, she
was overlooked by the boys. Only later, at sixth form,
when someone took a risk with her at a party, did she
get a decent press. The boys she had been with started
off kissing her as if they were doing her a great
favour. Bra off, their eyes would pop out of their
heads. By the time they were creaming themselves
over her incredible curves, they were in love with her.
But still that stigma remained.

She felt like pissing in their tea and kicking their
cameras over. Who cared if she got the sack? She
could clean school toilets and still earn more than
this.

Teeth grinding, she took a tray with their drinks
back to the warehouse proper. And almost dropped it.

Saffy was naked, spreadeagled on a cardboard box
filled with lever-arch files. Neil and Guy were standing over her, shirtless, dressed in blue serge trousers
and jackets, peaked caps and black boots. Guy's heavy,
coffee-coloured prick was bent down into Saffy's
mouth like a piece of flexible piping. Glimpses of his
shockingly pink core slipped into view as Saffy tried
her best to keep her lips fastened to his slippery,
sizeable girth. Neil was squatting between Saffy's
legs, his thighs shaking as they took the strain. He
was sawing the underside of his rigid cock, tip to root
and back again, along Saffy's juicy slot. Now and
again he dipped his helmet into her folds, but did not
penetrate her fully. She moaned at this teasing, and
tried, unsuccessfully, to feed him deeper into her by
wrapping her long legs around his buttocks.

Hector Furst watched it all through the viewfinder, occasionally muttering orders to the threesome: 'Ginger it up.' 'Throat it, Saf.' 'Pinch her nips, come on, let's see her stiffen.'

Suki put down the tray and considered going back to her little corner until they'd finished what they were doing, until Johnny Locke came along and sacked her or gave her a rise, or whatever the hell was going to happen. But she was transfixed. The pages of her magazine seemed to have come alive. And seeing so much sudden life within those heavy, boring uniforms was a real shock, a welcome one at that. Guy's tree-trunk legs made the fabric shiny where he was bulging against it. The contrast between the corded, dark texture of the jacket and Neil's smooth, willowy chest was breathtaking. The gleam of the caps' peaks was mirrored in the slicks of sweat spreading beneath them. And, under it all, tiny Saffy gulped down Guy's monster schlong, ground herself against Neil's solid curve and massaged her own yummy breasts until her nipples were sore from all the attention.

I'm her equal, Suki thought. She ticked off every department that she and the other woman shared and found that, apart from Saffy's legs (which were longer) and her face (amazing cheekbones, bee-stung lips, soft brown eyes), Suki was not wanting. I've got you beat on boobs, bum and bush, girl, she thought, and then, horribly, as the faces of Neil, Guy, Hector and, finally, bemusedly, Saffy, turned her way, she realised she had not thought the words at all. She had spoken them out loud.

'It's a little late for a screen test,' Hector said. 'And as I've stressed, time is money. But you ... what,

exactly? You feel you can improve our outfit here?
You want to add your spice to the recipe? Or is it just
the desperate squeak of a little bird, a plain little
sparrow who believes she is a dove at heart?'

'Give her a chance, Heck,' Saffy said, and Suki loved
her for it, wished she hadn't been so harsh in her
demeaning of the other woman. Still, she didn't know
quite what she was letting herself in for, or what she
ought to do. Her uniform never felt so uncomfortable.
It bit at her all over her body, prickling, pinching,
chafing.

'Come on then, little bird,' Furst said. 'Sing for me.'

'What do you want?' she asked.

'*Everything*,' Furst leered. 'But first, that tea. And a
little breaking of ice, yes?'

She sipped her tea sitting next to Saffy and apologised
for her outburst. 'I don't know what came over me,'
she said. 'Just job frustration, I suppose. I feel as
though I could do something much more interesting
than being a stupid nightwatchman. But I never seem
to get any opportunities.'

'Well, there's one staring you in the face now, isn't
there?' Saffy said. She had not dressed to enjoy her
tea break; she sat on the edge of a table, swinging her
long, bare legs, one arm folded under her pert, gravity-
defying breasts with their soft, pale-aubergine nipples
– the kind that Suki's mother had always referred to
as 'sit up and pay attention boobs' – and her tiny pot
belly with a simple steel bolt through the navel.

Neil, Guy and Hector were investigating the
darkest corners of the warehouse, looking for props or
locations that would elevate the film into something
out of the ordinary. By the time Hector came back

with three black truncheons, some handcuffs and the frame of a small metal bed, Suki was confident to say of Saffy that she was a friend.

'Film's called *Smash and Grab*, Suki,' Hector said. 'Here's the story. As you've already seen, Saffy's been taken into custody by our two manly nightwatchmen here, having been found trespassing on private property. Next scene, the scene where you come in, she's been delivered to the big boss, the ultra-disciplinarian bitch from hell, who just happens to be an insatiable nympho-slut with a taste for woman flesh. That's you, by the way. Thing is, she can only get her rocks off if said woman is yelling for mercy. So the way I see it is this: interrogation scene. Guy and Neil will busk things to start off with, get Saffy prepped, and then you, Suki, will come on and do what comes naturally. Let's see how you steal this scene from the others.'

Furst had lined up a couple of portable heaters and trained them on the roughly assembled scenery: the bed was padlocked to a heating pipe in a shabby, unadorned corner. Through the viewfinder, it looked exactly like a cell. No scripts were consulted, no motivation sought.

'You do what I say,' Hector said. 'That's all there is to it.'

Saffy was gently handcuffed to the bed, a gag wrapped around her mouth. Everyone smiled at her and asked if she was comfortable. Suki was touched by their concern for her and looked forward to a little bit of attention being paid to her. It had been a long time since anybody lavished that level of affection on her. Neil and Guy paced around Saffy like panthers until Hector said: 'OK, we're rolling. Action.' Guy unzipped himself, took out his cock and began to slowly masturbate himself hard. Saffy arched on the bed, her eyes large, at the same time looking as though she wanted to escape and yet equally desired what the two men were about to serve up to her.

Neil stood over Saffy's head and lowered his gear onto her face, smearing his swelling prick and balls against her nose and lips, causing her nostrils to flare with mild panic when she was momentarily unable to take a breath. He leaned over and roughly sucked her nipples awake, the large areolae gathering up into nubbled peaks that he hassled further with his teeth and tongue. His sucks and slurps flicked a switch in Suki's knickers. She felt herself moisten, as Saffy groaned beneath his tireless mouth. Neil reached down and cupped Saffy's neatly shaved mound, rotated his palm slowly until Saffy was pressing against him, seeking the entry of his fingers. The chains slinked against the metal bed frame; the sound of serge rubbing against itself as rhythms were found was like lazy wasps coming and going in a summer breeze. The polished peaks of their caps flashed as they turned their heads this way and that, observing Saffy's body and the things being done to it.

The heat increased. The three actors began to sweat. Saffy's body developed a glaze that gleamed and winked under the lights. At one point she turned her heavy, pleasure-loaded cat eyes Suki's way and winked drunkenly at her. Suki licked her lips. She wondered when she would be given the signal to enter stage right.

Guy had lifted Saffy's legs up so that they were vertical, making a right angle to the rest of her body. He placed them against his chest, the feet either side of his face. Without ceremony he plunged one of the black, shiny truncheons into the ripe split of her sex, which had been thrust plumply out between her closed thighs. Saffy howled around the gag and squeezed her eyes shut. She reached out and grabbed Neil's tool, began pumping it hard. Her face was red, lashed with damp curls. Guy found an instant, punishing rhythm that painted the truncheon with her fluids and sent a wet, slapping echo beating around the warehouse. Saffy's moans as she thrashed against Guy's pistoning action were having a positive effect on Hector Furst too: Suki saw his crotch begin to resemble a tent being assembled.

He said: 'OK, Suki. Do your worst.'

She stepped into the frame and put her hands on her hips, slung one out to the side. She knew how curvy she was; she knew how sexy this pose looked on her. She reached up and undid the clasp keeping her hair tied and knew how good the cascade of blonde hair against the blue serge at her back would look on film. She bellowed at Neil and Guy: 'Keep up the interrogation. She'll break before too long.'

She strode over to the bed and ran her hand down the slick, quivering tautness of Saffy's thigh. She stood behind Guy and got him to replace the truncheon with his own cock, pressed her hands against his buttocks and dipped a hand underneath to feel his pendulous balls as they slapped against Saffy's sodden perineum. She crouched by Neil, whose head was thrown back as Saffy's expert hand action drew every morsel of pleasure to the bulging purple bulb trapped in her fist. Suki rolled her tongue around it, created a drawbridge of saliva from his tip to her teeth. Her sex felt swollen with need. She felt that if someone were to touch her there she would drown the world with her moisture.

Everything she did was driven by instinct, and yet measured by what would look good on film, or what was visible. She never once stood between the lens and the action. She was on auto-pilot, yet aware of angles, space, aesthetics. She was a natural. She was thrilled that what she had been steaming up over in her magazine was suddenly being played out for real, with her at the centre of it all. The uniform of the nightwatchman suddenly possessed the authority and power that she had never believed invested in it before. She felt it stretch against her thighs, her breasts, her belly. She felt its seams empowering the V of her sex, could almost see her own oysterish folds delineated within the thick, rugged material. She squeezed her legs together, got a little motion going, felt the vibration of the narrow corded fabric, heard its busy little buzz. Her cunt lips meshed together like oiled silk.

She removed her jacket and clip-on tie. She pushed her arms inside the orbit of her braces and flipped them away, unbuttoned her blouse and pulled that off too. Back on with the braces, each strap pushed outwards slightly by the fine curve of her breasts: nipples concealed. She repositioned her cap so that the peak created a shadow that hid the upper half of her face. Just her wide, crimson-streaked mouth was visible. A half-turn to let the camera pick up on her lush profile, then she picked up her tie and approached Saffy.

Hector's voice: 'Oh, am I liking what I'm seeing very fucking much!'

She pushed Neil and Guy gently out of the way, enjoying the way they bowed slightly to give the impression of rank, and stood looking down at Saffy.

Her face bore disappointment. She lowered her legs and her tuft of pubic hair glistened with all the juices she'd leaked.

'You *will* talk,' Suki said, forbiddingly, and pressed open the spring-loaded crocodile clip at the back of the knot of her tie. A plain black tie that was suddenly the focus of everyone in the room. Saffy's eyes widened with pleasure and apprehension as she realised what was about to happen. Suki winked at her as she positioned the teeth of the clip on either side of Saffy's left nipple. Then she let go. Saffy's moan was like something being birthed, some magnificent, dark bird releasing itself of the fabric of fantasy. Suki thought she saw even the shadows quake as it reverberated around the massive space. Saffy's face had contorted into a mask of concentration. Her lips had turned ruddy and her cheeks bloomed two high punches of colour. She lifted her buttocks clear of the boxes and parted her legs. Hector raced around with his camera trained on her pussy.

'She's coming. Christ, girl, she's coming.'

Saffy's hips bucked twice, three times, and a clear jet of fluid dashed from her quim. Neil and Guy, momentarily stunned by this occurrence, quickly got back into character and homed in on Saffy's writhing body to avail themselves of its bountiful fruits. Suki peeled off Saffy's gag; she was still coming down from her climax. 'Oh, God, that was good. That was *so* good.' Suki stepped out of her braces again, unfastened her trousers and knickers and stood naked in front of everybody. She saw Neil and Guy trade looks and heard Hector's breath catch in his throat. She was like something that could only be measured in sine waves.

'More curves than an Aston Martin,' Neil said, reaching out to stroke her breasts, which jiggled slightly under his fingers.

Suki bent over Saffy's face and kissed her, upside down, on the mouth. She took her time over it. She had never kissed a woman before and wondered at the tenderness of it, the fullness of the lips. She felt Saffy's sweet little tongue dab at her own like a curious fish. When she broke away, Saffy smiled at her. Suki leaned further over and allowed her breasts to drag sensuously across Saffy's hair, forehead and face. She clenched her hands together as she felt Saffy's mouth suck and kiss her nipples erect and returned the favour, turning circles with her tongue around Saffy's beautiful globes. Still she moved on, encouraged by Saffy's hungry mouth, stopping only when she felt Saffy's tongue slip into her bush and flicker at her clit. She closed her eyes and felt herself being almost reshaped inside, so intense were the sensations. When she opened them again, Guy was standing in front of her, his feet on either side of Saffy's belly. His large cock was waving in front of her face, millimetres from her mouth. 'Hi,' he said.

'Hi,' she replied, and happily wolfed it down, wondering what had happened to their interrogation scene. Hector was no longer barking orders. She glanced his way, having to shift her head slightly to see around Guy's thrusting hips, but Hector had gone, the camera on its tripod drinking in their details alone. She was too blissed out on what was happening to her to care. She let Guy fuck her mouth, greedily sucking him as deeply as she was able, before she was aware of Neil, who had crawled between the V of Guy's legs. He was athletically fucking Saffy now, missionary style, and taking it in turns lapping at Saffy's and Suki's breasts. Saffy's hands were coaxing Guy's balls. There were limbs everywhere. She felt a change of pace, of intent. She felt her insides grow so hot she couldn't work out where her pussy and Saffy's mouth were divisible. She felt herself beginning to lose control, her bum and thighs trembling uncontrollably. Guy's head was thrown back; she could make out the cords on his neck. She wrapped her braces tight around the base of his dick until the veins stood out. Her nose mashed against the reinforced serge flaps of his fly as he rammed himself home for the final time and she felt his end twitch, his arse turn as stiff as two bricks and what felt like a half a pint of come explode into her mouth. She tried hard to breathe and swallow and let him loose gently as her own orgasm blistered through her. Neil was next, pulling out to shoot his load across Saffy's belly and thighs. Commas of seed splashed against his heavy work trousers, the material too dense to absorb it. The stack of bodies collapsed deliciously into a soft/hard mass. A little time helped to soften it further, to slow breathing, to remove the red colour from cheeks and chests. Gradually the limbs disentangled. Nobody spoke.

Until Suki realised that, somehow, her wrist was wearing a handcuff, and it was fastened to the frame of the bed.

'Sorry,' Saffy said, and ducked to kiss her on the cheek.

'Sorry,' Neil said, and ruffled her hair.

'Sorry,' Guy said, stuffing his beautiful prick back inside his trousers.

'Johhny's not coming, is he?' Suki asked, as Hector

reappeared from the office, his hands clutching two large bags of cash, harvested from the safe in the wall. His mirror shades were gone now and she realised where she recognised him from. This very building, only instead of money bags in his hands, he usually carried a mop, or a broom, or a can of Pledge.

'No,' he said. 'But we left you a little something. To say thanks.

And then they were gone. There was just her, and the bed, and a couple of discarded uniforms, a camera running without any tape to record what had, she was forced to admit, been a very interesting little crime.

She managed eventually to pull one of the bed's legs apart and the handcuff securing it to the pipe fell free. She dragged what was left of the frame across to the office where she had seen Hector leave the keys. A few minutes of struggling with the bed as she tried to get through the door and she was able to release herself. She stood in the office, rubbing her wrists, and stared at the open safe. The envelope sticking out was like a tongue mocking her. But that image disappeared instantly the moment she opened it and found a photograph and £3,000.

The next day, after the police had taken her (fictionalised) statement, she was summoned to Johnny Locke's office. She stood before her boss's desk as Johnny carpeted her, his face running a gamut of colours that started with puce and finished near black. His voice had carried so much rage that she was sure she saw the windows tremble. Spittle flew from his lips like rice at a wedding. Only this was nothing like such a happy event. This was its diametric opposite. This was a divorce in every way. The words rained down on her: fired, sacked, terminated, OUT OUT OUT.

She took a deep breath and smiled serenely at him. Her navy-blue serge uniform whispered softly against her empowered curves. The day before, although a sham, had instilled her with courage, confidence and belief in her own sexuality. The man before her, as much as he bellowed, was a speck in comparison. Her smile broadened. She said, 'I don't think so.'

Locke said: 'Excuse me?'

'I want to stay in the job. In fact, I want a raise. A very big raise. In fact, I want what you earn.'

'Do you want me to physically pick you up and kick you into the gutter?' The puce was returning.

'I'll let you keep your job,' she said. 'But I want things to change. Starting . . . now.'

She let the photograph in her hand flutter down to his table. His eyes remained on hers for a second, then twitched to the 5×7 rectangle. She never would have believed that a simple photograph could make someone's eyes grow so large. Then again, whose eyes wouldn't bulge if their owner was wearing the kind of butt plug that wore feathers, tasted great with roast potatoes and maybe couldn't ask you how you wanted your eggs but could at least lay them for you instead.

'It's a colour print,' Suki said. 'But it looks like black and white to me.'

Nuala Deuel is the co-author of *Princess Spider: True Experiences of a Dominatrix*, and has had short fiction published in numerous Wicked Words collections.

Precipitous Passions
Michelle M Pillow

'You can't deny that you want me to fuck you.'

'Excuse me?' Hallie asked, unsure she had heard him right. She swung around from the top edge of the New York skyscraper. Her round green eyes widened in shock as her short blonde curls bounced excitedly in the wind. She immediately recognised the voice as that of her boss Peter Bartlett; he was the only one she knew with such a sharp British accent. He was also the only one she knew with keys to the rooftop door, aside from the janitor whose set she had borrowed. His perfectly formed words could give any American girl chills. But surely he would not make such a blatantly sexual remark? Theirs was a working relationship, tempered by the mix of a little humour and stoic attitudes, although they had always gotten along in the most proper of workplace senses.

Hallie peered through the soft glow of fluorescent lights that lined the edge of the building and questioned uneasily, 'Mr Bartlett?'

'Call me Peter. We're off the clock.' He flashed a quizzically boyish smile as he answered casually, 'And you cannot deny that you would miss out on this view. New York is one of the most fabulous cities in the world. I should know. I've seen most of them.'

'Oh,' Hallie said, turning her eyes to the dim sky

blazing with the light fog of the bright city night. The top of the Harrison and Kenton office building was a perfect spot to see the city. The skyline was indeed beautiful – the most untamed spot in the New York. She was careful not to look down, lest her stomach lurch with unease. Standing on this part of the roof was perilous; one false step and you could fly to your death.

But Hallie liked the freedom of the roof; it was why she visited it often. It resembled a wild sense of freedom and longing within her. She was normally tame, cautious. Here, the world looked so big and alive, and she felt like ruling it all.

Hearing her boss near her, she wanted to melt into the stone in embarrassment; her cheeks flamed with the mortification at her wayward thoughts. Her only redemption was that Peter couldn't read her dirty mind. She felt him lean next to her on the railing, could feel the heat of his body as he stood close yet not quite touching. Ignoring the flush that threatened her skin, she managed to respond after some time.

'I suppose it's much more exotic when you haven't lived here forever.'

'Why does every American woman dream of Paris?' He chuckled in amusement. 'Yours wasn't the only application I had to rifle through this last week. Every girl in the office put in for the overseas job.'

'I'm not sure why,' she lied, turning to go as a strong breeze whipped sharply over her flushed skin. It ruffled the neckline of her white linen shirt, exposing her bare throat and a hint of the top of a lacy bra. His eyes caught hers in a brief grasp before they dipped lower to glance at the exposure of curved cleavage. Suddenly she wished she hadn't unbuttoned the stuffy collar. Weakly, she said, 'I should really be going. The meeting will be over soon and Mr Kenton is leaving some paperwork on my desk.'

'Always working late, aren't you, Hallie? It is nearly eleven o'clock.' Peter's words weren't really a question but a deliberate pondering. He drew his eyes away and Hallie forced herself to relax. 'Don't you ever go out for fun?'

'Are you giving me permission to call in sick tomorrow?' she asked with a sheepish smile. 'Mr Kenton will be sorely disappointed if the modified reports aren't on his desk first thing in the morning.'

'Do you always do as you're told?' His mouth barely moved as he murmured the low question. Hallie felt a chill over her skin and convinced herself it was the wind.

'Only when it's one of my bosses doing the telling,' she quipped matter-of-factly. 'I won't lie. I want that Paris job. I'm one of the hardest workers you've got down there and –'

'Hallie,' Peter broke in, giving a small shake of his head as he stopped her words with the softness of his tone. 'Save it for the interviews.'

'Sorry,' she said with an apologetic smile she didn't mean. 'Like I said, I've got to get back to work.'

She turned to go, unable to take his unfamiliar nearness. The whole of New York didn't seem big enough for the both of them, as they stood facing each other on the empty roof. Her fingers worked uneasily with a will of their own, wanting to feel where Peter's T-shirt moulded to his strong chest. She could smell his scent, purely masculine, as it drifted to her in diluted waves, filling her senses.

Taking slow steps towards the door, she forced

herself not to run. The image of his unusually casual attire burned into her mind, though she had tried hard not to look at him. Peter was her boss. During the day, everything was all business with him. Never had he given the slightest impression that he was attracted to her. Hell, he never gave her the impression he even really liked her. But tonight, on the roof of their office building, things were about to change. Had she imagined it? Were the powerful night air and the dizzyingly spellbinding influence of the tall building and surrounding city playing tricks on her?

'I've seen the way you've been looking at me,' he said.

Hallie froze, her back turned to him, sure that her mind was again playing tricks on her. She had misheard him. He couldn't know what she thought of him, how she thought of him. Rotating slowly on her high heels, she said, 'I'm sorry? I didn't hear you over the wind.'

Suddenly his mood changed. His arms moved with the assurance and certainty of his perfect body. 'Don't you ever say what you want? Why do you play all these coy games?'

He smiled in devilish enjoyment. His T-shirt again sculpted to his muscled chest. It glowed eerily in the combination of moonlight and fluorescence. His short black hair ruffled defiantly in the breeze, as confident as its master as the locks pushed over his brow.

'Games?' she squeaked. Her pulsed raced. She couldn't read his face. She didn't recognise the man before her.

'You want me,' he persisted. 'Sexually. I can see that you do. I have always seen it.'

Hallie shook her head in denial, embarrassed by the truth in his words. She had wanted him from the first moment she saw him standing in the boardroom, introducing himself to the company. But the jolt of that first encounter had faded into a dull ache of vague disappointment when he returned nothing but a passing interest. Even now, she couldn't read any fondness in his face.

'Be honest,' he continued. 'For once, tell me the truth.'

'Why?'

'Let us just say I'm curious.' When she merely lifted an eyebrow, he added, 'Whoever we send to Paris needs to be bold. Mr Kenton wants to hire a man. He thinks woman are too timid to lead a company.'

'I don't want to lose my job,' she bit off tersely. Mr Kenton was an old-school chauvinist. Had he sent Peter to test her? Lifting her chin, she decided feigning irritation was better than admitting she was attracted to Peter's stiffly charming smile and hard, dark eyes.

'You won't,' he promised. 'Tell me what you think of me.'

'You exasperate me. You are domineering and cold. You never smile and are sparse with praise. If anything, I have been silently glaring at you in irritation.' Hallie took a step away from his perusing glances. His eyes raked over her form in a way she had never seen him look at her. After a long moment, his gaze took in her short black skirt.

'So you aren't attracted to me?' he questioned. The tip of his tongue darted playful over the lower line of his lip. A challenge lit on his face as his full mouth curled into a dangerous smile. His eyes dared her to lie to him.

'No,' she said. Hallie lifted her chin proudly into the air. Her heart beat in wild thumps. Yelling as the wind picked up, she hollered, 'I can't stand you.'

'I don't believe you. Your body language says otherwise.'

Hallie stood transfixed. She couldn't run. She was excited as she listened for his next words. She followed his movements, noticing his hand as it lifted from his waist to pass over his rising cock in a steady massage, drawing her gaze to the bulge to emphasise his meaning. A fire shot through her limbs. Her body jolted to life, begging her hips to gyrate in the air, crying out for her hands to tear away clothing that felt too constrictive.

'And I'd bet I could smell it on you if I were to press my nose between your legs,' Peter said.

'Is that why you followed me up here? You think I wanted you?' Hallie refused to back away from him again. His thumb deftly unbuttoned his fly. She again caught the musty scent of his cologne on the stout breeze. The rooftop dimmed all but the man before her. 'Don't think for a second that I wanted you to.'

'No?' he questioned. He cracked a smile as she shook her curly head. 'Then give me one minute of your time. If you are not crying out in passion by then, I'll leave you alone.'

Hallie frowned in disbelief. She had been caught out by the truth and was burning was a mixture of shame and arousal. As he came up to look her steadily in the eye, she shivered. She was already moist from his bold proposal. Pleasure hummed through her, running rampant in her veins, sparking her nerves to life. But it was a hateful tease on his part to get her body singing to such an extent.

'Is this a test?' she breathed, her voice raspy as she tried her best to control it. 'Are you trying to see if I will do anything to get the Paris job? I'll have you know I've more than proved myself as qualified. I'm one of the highest ranked associates in this whole city.'

'I am testing you,' he admitted. 'But not for Paris.'

'Then –'

'I'm testing your control, Hallie. How tightly do you have that body of yours reined in? How tight are the ropes of your sexuality? Let me untie them. Let me untie you. If you don't enjoy it, I'll quit my job and never bother you again,' he whispered near her ear. His heated breath tickled her skin.

'Really?' she asked, knowing full well that men will say anything to get into a woman's panties. Her breasts heaved with a heavy sigh. Her lips parted in expectation.

'I promise,' he murmured huskily. He touched her shoulder and lightly ran his hand over her shivering arm.

The idea had merit. Peter had been an aggravating pain in her ass since he took over her department three months ago. Still, she knew she shouldn't believe him; he was just a horny man trying to get laid. He had never come on to her before. Peter wasn't really attracted to her, was he?

'You're a pain in my ass,' she said. 'You are aware of that, are you not?'

At that his smile deepened. Taking the tip of his finger, he traced it boldly over the line of her nipple as it peaked under her shirt. Hallie trembled.

'I could be.' He smirked. Slowly he began to circle around her. When he reached her ass, he grabbed it and squeezed. Hallie stepped away from him. Again he came up behind her before she could turn around. This time the firm outline of his penis pressed into her soft cleft. She jolted in surprise. She never would have guessed Peter to be so well-endowed.

Belatedly, she tried to pull away but his hand shot over her stomach to stop her. Her head whirled in confusion. Peter's flat palm slid lower to hover over her sex. How was this happening? Only in her darkest dreams had she thought about this moment. And yet, here it was, pressing between the cheeks of her ass.

Peter leaned over to whisper darkly in her ear, not giving her time to think or reason. 'Why won't you admit you want me to fuck you? You want me inside of you. I can sense it. You're wet and aching through your black skirt, aren't you?' Moving to her other ear, he lightly licked the sensitive nub with a quick dash of his tongue. 'Your pussy's begging my long, hard cock to release it. Bend over for me, Hallie, feel my cock. Let me take you here and now on the side of this building. Let me ride you.'

'So what if I am aroused? It doesn't mean I want you.' Hallie made a pathetic attempt to try and pull away. The height of the building combined with his sexual advances made her dizzy. He sensed the game, and wouldn't let her go. Trying to be as bold as he, she stated, 'And I don't wish to feel your cock anywhere near me.'

Peter chuckled, disbelieving. He reached his free hand to caress her neck before dipping his callused palm into the top of her blouse. It found a home in the valley of her breasts. Pulling her body harder against him, he ground his hips slowly against the cheeks of her ass. He felt her body stir in desire. He could feel her growing heat as he stoked her inner flame, leaving a trail of goosebumps in his wake. Her heart pounded wildly against his fingertips.

'You're aroused,' he said in a breathy hush along the nape of her neck. Lightly, he began to kiss her creamy skin. 'I'm horny.'

'Your emotions are not my problem,' Hallie put forth as she ripped his hand from her shirt. She threw his fingers from her. Twisting away from him, she ignored his groan of discontentment. 'Now, Mr Bartlett, if you'll excuse me –'

'You can't escape. The door's locked,' Peter said quietly from behind her. His hands strayed to his hips. The dark orbs of his eyes glared in annoyance at her withdrawal. 'And that janitor key won't open it.'

Hallie marched to the door. She hadn't seen him come up so didn't realise he had locked her out of the building. The only other way down was over the side – a seventy-two-storey fall.

Hallie swung around to face him. By now he had taken off his T-shirt and stood proudly before her. She caught her breath at his rippling muscled form. Swallowing hard, she said, 'You can't keep me here.'

'Can't I?' he smirked.

'You have no right to take me prisoner.'

'You're not my prisoner ... yet.'

'Mr Bartlett –' she began in stern warning. But, even as her words were hard, her eyes were aflame. They dipped over his chest, focusing on his cock.

'Didn't you say you always listened to your boss?' he questioned logically.

'Yes, I did, but –'

'If you don't listen to me, listen to your body.'

Hallie stood silent. She was terrified – terrified of

the passion inside her. This was Peter. It wasn't a good idea to get involved with one's boss. No matter how badly she wanted it to happen, it could ruin her career.

'Fine, then come and get the key and unlock the door,' he said when she held silent. His words were harshly delivered but a gleam entered his wicked eyes.

'Where is it?' she stammered.

'Hidden in a very safe place,' he said. Then with a cheeky glance he motioned to his protruding trousers. 'Though you are most welcome to try and find it.'

'Don't think I won't,' Hallie said, trying to intimidate him. Inside she shivered with lust.

'I won't stop you,' he paused meaningfully. With a flick of his fingers he unzipped his blue jeans, before continuing, 'But I must insist you use your mouth.'

That stopped her. Turning from him with uncertainty, she took a deep breath. The more he spoke, the more she wanted to forget decorum and fuck his brains out. But this was Peter she had to remind herself – her irritating boss who hardly said two words to her unless it was to criticise her work.

'Why are you doing this now?' she asked.

'Why not now?' he answered.

'We have been working together for three months. You have never shown interest before.'

'I've been waiting to get you alone,' Peter answered.

'We have been alone in your office plenty.' Hallie turned around to face him, sure that she could keep her face composed. Her eyes automatically drifted to his crotch. His pants hugged at his tapered waist in a snug fit.

'I thought about it,' he admitted. 'I've thought about it a lot. Especially at night, with a raging hard-on.'

'Then?'

'There are too many distractions in the office during the day. My office door doesn't lock. Janice always walks in unannounced.' He took small steps as he spoke. Hallie stood enthralled by his low, husky voice. 'How would she like it to find you bent over my desk with my dick in your ass?'

'You could have said something.' Hallie licked her lips. 'There were other times.'

'When?' he questioned urgently. 'You always work late.'

'You could have said something.' Her resolve continued to slip. Silently, she wondered, Why not take him into her mouth? Why not control him for once? Who would know?

'Yes, I could have. I could have asked you out on a proper date, took you to a fine restaurant. But I don't want a date. I want to fuck you. I want you to suck my rock-hard cock. I want to bend you over and taste your wet pussy.' Peter stopped in front of her, letting his bold words sink in. 'I want to lean you over the side of this building and –'

'But –'

'And,' he began again with impassioned emphasis. 'I want to shove my dick in your hot and willing body.'

'Peter,' she stated with a blush fanning her cheeks. 'Who put you up to this? This is an office dare, right? Everyone is hiding behind the door, listening.'

'Would you like it if they were?' he asked. 'Would it excite you to have them watch?'

'No,' she stammered. The lie was obvious.

'Who would you like to join us? Gladys from copying? My secretary, Janice? Your secretary, Stephen?' He pulled the phone from his pocket, and smiled as he shook it at her. 'I could call them. Tell them to come up here for an emergency meeting.'

'That's preposterous,' Hallie shot in confusion.

'No, I've seen the way Stephen looks at your ass. I've seen you bend over a little extra when he is around to let him.' Peter laughed when she pinked in slight embarrassment. 'Tell me, have you had him yet?'

'Of course not.'

'Have you called him into your office? Taken off your panties and sat on your desk while making him eat you out?' Peter persisted.

'No,' Hallie said, barely able to believe the way her boss was speaking to her.

'But you want to, don't you? Between us, admit it. You want the power of being in charge. That is what really attracts you to Paris. You want complete control.' Peter eyed her lips. His words fanned over her in a low, seductive murmur. 'Be a woman – admit it.'

'Fine, I admit it. I've thought of him naked. I've thought about almost every man in the office naked. It doesn't mean I would act on it. It's human nature to be curious,' Hallie said.

'Shall I tell you what I would think about when you come into my office? Shall I tell you what I've been waiting to do to you?' Peter looked unashamedly at her breasts as they coloured with her excited breath. 'Shall I tell you how you affect me?'

Unable to stop herself, Hallie nodded.

Peter smiled that devilishly wicked grin that made her flesh tingle.

'As you would speak, rattling on about financial proposals and stock options I would stare at your mouth. I'd imagine jumping over the desk and sticking my cock in your face, making you talk around it until I came in your throat. As you spoke I would secretly masturbate under my desk, asking you questions so you wouldn't stop moving your lush, full lips. And I'd stare at your breasts, perky and round as they moved under your blouse, wondering what kind of bra you had worn for me that day.'

Peter grabbed her by the arm, and this time she didn't move. His low voice entranced her as he spoke forbidden words of passion. Gently, he raised his fingers to her blouse and undid a button, letting the breeze pull apart the material to discover her lacy white bra. His eyes narrowed, his breath deepened.

It amazed Hallie that he'd thought of her in such a way. But she read the truth of it in his wildly fervent eyes.

Continuing, he said, 'I've often wondered...' He paused to press a kiss on her exposed collarbone. Licking her chest in a long hot stroke, he trailed up her neck to claim her parted lips.

'What?' she breathed in a low murmur when he almost kissed her.

Moving his lips lightly against her mouth, he said, 'Are you as hot as I want you to be?'

She pulled back. 'Now you're just teasing me. Game's over, Peter, give me the key. I've got to go. I've got a long hard day tomorrow.'

'I've got a long hard night for you here,' he shot back just as smoothly.

He took her hand and held it to his cock. She jerked away.

'Let me show it to you.'

Hallie froze, curiosity causing her to look down to his exposed black silk boxers. He pulled back his fly, groaning slightly when his dick sprung free. Hallie licked her trembling lips. Her eyes grew wide with interest. Tilting her head to the side, she stared at his protrusion, waiting for him to pull it free from its silken prison.

He stroked himself over the silk, starting deep at the base before slowly moving to the head of his shaft. Unbidden, Hallie's hand strayed to the valley between her breasts.

'Just pretend you have to work late,' Peter said. He massaged himself again with a groan. 'I'll tell Kenton I kept you late and the report won't be done until noon.'

'How late?'

'I just might keep you here all night.' Grinning, he asked, 'How many times can you orgasm?'

'Depends on how good the man is,' she said with a matching smile.

'I'm good.' Peter lifted a hand to undo another of her buttons. He growled when he laid bare her heaving chest. 'Let me taste your skin.'

He didn't wait for her to answer. Leaning over he licked the valley of her breasts. Then, trailing his caressing lips over the edge of her bra he dipped his tongue underneath the thin material to lap her pointed nipple. Hallie gasped and her knees weakened as she stumbled back. Peter smiled and caught her. She fell to press against the hard metal door.

'You're trapped,' he told her. He placed his hands on either side of her head. Looking down at her chest, he moistened his lips. 'You need a man to free you.'

'I –'

'Shhh,' Peter hushed. 'It's all right. A lot of women haven't been with a man secure enough in himself to give her real pleasure. I can feel the hesitation in your body. You're scared of me. You're scared of what I am offering you.'

'And just what are you offering?' she threw back.

'Pure –' he stopped to kiss the rapid pulse at her neck, '– pleasure without any commitments or attachments. No phone calls to make the next morning or awkward moments after. Just a good, solid fucking and no one will ever have to know unless you want them to.'

Hallie's breath deepened as his lips continued a reckless course over her tender flesh. The hard metal door pressed into her skin, holding her steady in the strong wind blowing over the skyscraper's roof. Her heart raced in excitement as she anticipated being discovered. She imagined someone listening on the other side of the thick steel.

The movement of his bold lips entranced her and his body shielded her from the harsh glow of the rooftop's fluorescent lights. Behind his head she saw the dim poke of stars as a helicopter flew in the distance. Her will slipped and she felt him taking over.

'Spread your legs, Hallie,' he commanded. 'Open them up for me.'

Hesitantly she complied. Parting her thighs under the tight black skirt, she moved her heeled shoes to the side. Peter chuckled as his hands rose from the door to touch her slender frame. He caressed her body in long, worshiping strokes. Slowly, he made his way down to her hips to kneel before her.

'Lift your skirt,' he ordered.

Hallie shivered. Following the trail he had blazed over her body, she moved to touch the hem of her skirt. Her hands trembled, unsure.

'Show yourself to me,' he growled harshly. 'Now.'

Hallie obeyed. She was so wet, so hot. Her hands grasped the fine material and slowly began to lift it.

Peter avidly watched the unveiling of her athletic thighs. Her skirt inched higher to show the rim of her white lace panties covering her mound of trimmed blonde hair.

'More!' he demanded fiercely. 'Show me your pussy. Show me how hot it is for me.'

Growing empowered by his attention, she slowly inched the skirt higher. The thin straps of her panties hugging her hips came into view. The cool night breeze caressed her skin. She felt powerful, conquering, as if she were on top of the world.

Peter grabbed her hips, his thumbs hooked under the thin straps. He sniffed delightedly in the air. Hoarsely, he said, 'Touch yourself for me. Make yourself moist with desire. I want to watch you give yourself pleasure.'

Hallie followed his instructions, unable to resist her body's longing. Her flesh swam with too many sensations not to comply. Placing a finely manicured hand on her flat stomach, she brought it down over her panties with agonising slowness. Pressing her middle finger into the lace to part her moistening lips, she moaned in delight.

'Go under,' he urged in a throaty command.

Once more she obeyed him. She raised her fingers and looped them inside the lacy barrier. His mouth moved closer to pant hotly on her thighs. His eyes bore into her, watching as she stroked herself. With a mischievous glint shining from his dark eyes, he raised his arms and pulled roughly at her blouse. The last clinging buttons caught in the wind and blew away as he ripped her shirt open. The wind hit her aching breasts and she ground her hips wantonly against her probing hand.

Peter touched her flesh in heated strokes, liking the way her heels lengthened her legs. His penis stirred in delight and strained to be free from the confines of silk. He wanted to push himself roughly into her, but held back; waiting was half the pleasure.

'Are you wet for me?' he asked.

'Mmm,' she hummed her assent.

'Are you hot for me?'

'Yes,' she answered in a tortured pant.

'Then show me,' he said grabbing her hips. 'Let me taste you.'

'OK,' she said. 'Taste me!'

With an almost inhuman growl, Peter ripped the panties down. The torn lace flew away in the wind, disappearing over the edge of the building. Her fingers kept up their agonising pace and he watched as her manicured nail rubbed the swollen nub of her clit. Her finger dipped inside her opening. Then, seeing a glint of metal, he licked his lips in playful surprise.

'You've got a piercing,' he said looking at the curved barbell hanging from the top of her arch. 'That excites me very much. I didn't think you would have been that type of girl.'

'What type is that?' she questioned in distraction. Her fingers continued to stroke, moving faster now that the panties no longer pressed into the back of her hand.

'My type,' Peter said.

He took the circular barbell into his lips, and sucked the metal ring in between his teeth. Hallie groaned in encouragement, her fingers stroking faster. Peter sucked his lips fully onto her cunt in an opened-mouth caress. Licking and lapping next to her fingers he pushed his tongue inside her moist velvet lips.

As the movements of his mouth became more pleasurable than those of her fingers, she tore her hand away and shoved them into his dark hair. Pressing at his head more insistently she thrust herself against his probing tongue. His pulled on her ring with his teeth and his tongue delved inside her, stroking keenly at her core. A rumbling growl escaped his lips, reverberating off her flesh like the fine-tuning of a vibrator.

Hallie yelled as she thrust her hips faster and faster. Peter grabbed one of her legs and threw it over his shoulder to better angle her to his searching mouth. She pressed his head into her cunt, smothering him with her slick juices.

He felt her tense in ecstasy then tasted the flow of her desire. He grabbed her hips, refusing to let her back away from his mouth as the pleasure began to shake in her body.

Hallie shouted her climax high into the night. They were surrounded by a city of millions and yet no one would hear her gratified cry. Peter pulled his mouth away with a delighted smirk. As her eyes flew down in wonder to look at him, he licked his lips. Slowly her leg fell back to the ground.

'I told you I could give you pleasure,' he said with a confident smirk.

Hallie grabbed her skirt and tugged it over her

hips. She smiled back playfully. 'Thanks, I needed that. Now can I have the key?'

'Oh no,' he said. 'We're not done.'

Peter looked down at his cock, still hard and straining with a violent need.

'I already told you,' Hallie said. 'You are not my problem.'

Peter grunted his denial as he shot up to grab her about the shoulders. He pressed himself into her black skirt. 'I am, if you ever want to get off this roof.'

Hallie grinned wickedly, taking control. Feeling liberated by the delight that still coursed in her veins, she pushed him backwards. Peter grew confused.

'Are you going to push me over the side?' he asked, unconcerned.

'I've thought about it,' Hallie answered coyly.

Peter's back hit the concrete of the building's wall. He placed his arms over the side to hold himself steady. Glancing down at his crotch, he said, 'Well, get the key if you want to leave.'

Hallie pressed her body near him.

'Use your mouth,' he said in a heated whisper.

Hallie drew her face close to his. She could smell the traces of her wetness on his lips. She kissed him, licking her tongue over his teeth.

'Kiss me lower,' he urged.

Her hand found his hard cock. She freed it from its black silk prison. Peter's eyes bored into her, urging as she fondled him. His hips ground into her hand, teased by the warmth of her palm and the contrasting coolness of the night air.

Hallie's torn blouse whipped behind her in the breeze. Her free hand moved over his smooth chest, caressing the rigid folds of muscle. Behind his head was the distant pattern of countless windows, some illuminated, but most as dark as night.

'I see you work out,' she commented with a coy smile.

'Suck me, Hallie,' he said, ignoring her appraisal of his physique and growing more insistent. His used his strength to push her to her knees before him. Holding her steady, he edged his hips to her tauntingly lush lips. 'Suck it, now.'

Hallie spread her knees apart, sensually thrusting her hips in the air as she licked lightly over the taut flesh of his cockhead. Peter's stomach tensed and flexed with excruciating torment. He gripped the ledge for support.

Hallie continued her gentle licks as she grabbed his jeans. Pulling them roughly down, she exposed his balls, smiled at his vulnerable position and took them in her hands. Squeezing gently, she elicited a moan of delight. Then, after trailing her lips over the length of his erection, Hallie took the large tip into her mouth.

Peter felt the moist slickness surround his shaft like the opening of a snug, moist cunt. Her teeth grazed him lightly; her hands stayed with his balls. Gripping the wall, he grimaced in satisfaction as she blew lightly and sucked heavily in turn. Nearly gagging her with his length, he thrust deeper within her throat. Then, as an orgasm approached, he pulled her roughly off.

Hallie looked up in surprise.

'You're much better at that than I would have thought,' Peter said. 'I should have had you beneath my desk rather than on the other side of it.'

'Let me finish it,' Hallie returned huskily. Her eyes were clouded with an aroused light. Opening her mouth, she hissed, 'Give me your cock. I want to make you come.'

'I'll give it to you,' he promised, 'but I don't want your mouth.'

'Then –' she began.

'Get up here and lean over this wall. Look over the edge,' Peter said.

Hallie obeyed. Unconcerned, she teased, 'Are you going to try and push me over?'

'Oh no,' Peter said laughing. 'Not before I've had my fun.' He forcibly spun her to face the stars and her head reeled back on her shoulders. Her vision swam with the wide night sky as the wind embraced her flesh. With a gently insistent push, he urged her head down over the edge of the building. Whispering hotly into her ear, he said, 'I have much more enjoyable tasks in mind for you and this soft body of yours.'

She braced herself more deftly against the concrete, and he came up behind her. Her stomach lurched, torn between the natural fear of being so vulnerably suspended and the excitement of Peter's forbidden touch. The ground became but a black hole beneath her vision, causing the blood to rush in her veins. Only the streetlights sprinkled the ground, bringing light to the darkness by mimicking the starry heavens.

Peter yanked her skirt up then slapped her exposed cheeks before roughly grabbing her hips. His strong fingers journeyed up the small of her back to press her more firmly forwards. Her skin scraped gently over concrete and her hair dangled towards the earth as she looked over the steep, unforgiving edge.

'Where would you like me?' he asked.

She was beyond caring. 'Put it wherever you want.'

Peter chuckled. Taking himself in hand, he rubbed his cock along the crack of her ass. Then, holding her still by force of will, he placed his hand possessively on her hips. With each word he spoke, he rubbed himself against her in a teasing caress.

'Is your cunt wet and hot for me?' he asked.

'Uh-huh,' she answered. She closed her eyes to the drop below.

'Do you want me to ride you with my enormous, hard cock?'

'Yeah.'

'Do you want to be fucked rough and strong?'

'Yes, do it!' Hallie commanded. 'Do it now! Fuck me!'

Peter guided his cock to the opened lips of her moist pussy. Instinctively knowing she had never taken it in the ass, he decided to begin simply and work his way up to it. The last thing he wanted was for her to back out.

'Hold on to the edge, baby,' he said.

'Do it!' she ordered in frantic persistence. 'Take your giant cock and stick it in me now! Fuck me! Claim me! Ride me hard!'

With stiff confidence he embedded himself deeply within her, prying her apart as he sank the whole of his thickened shaft inside her luxuriously wet passage. He had wanted her since the first moment he saw her in his boardroom, pouring coffee for some investors. And now he'd hit pay dirt.

Hallie bucked and shouted to the stars in noisy rapture before looking down the long drop of the skyscraper's outside wall. Her heart hammered at the dangerous thrill as Peter jabbed inside her, thrusting and pulling with unrestrained vigour. The heavy push of his engorged cock nudged her closer to the edge until her head was flying past the corner, only to be drawn back by the powerful strength of his hands on her hips. The rough stone of the building brushed up against the top curves of her breasts, snagging her lacy bra. The concrete kisses on her erect nipples sent chills over the aching tips to radiate through her.

Peter threw back his head in sheer ecstasy at the dominant force of his possession. His body controlled her passions, pushing her higher with every commanding plunge. Their movements became frenzied as he rode her like a wild man.

Hallie felt her body began to shake. Her stomach lurched and trembled in mounting gratification. Peter held back, taking his orgasm inside of himself so as not to lose his solid erection. He was not done with her yet.

Giving her only a moment to dwell in her pleasure, he moved his finger to the crack of her ass. He kept himself moving deeply inside of her cunt as his fingers sought reaction to his touch. Hallie tried to jerk away from him but he refused. Her body hummed with unsteady pleasure as Peter's thrust slowed by a small degree.

He controlled her completely and grew mad with the power of it. And as her trembling began to subside, he started to pump once more in his frenzied pace. Instantly, Hallie began to quiver in response to his hard persistence. She hollered in wicked delight.

In amazement, she felt her body tighten with a second orgasm. She cried out with the strength of it – the unexpected payoff for risking her life in this wild crazy moment. Her body went numb from the onslaught of pleasure. If not for his hold on her ass, she could be falling over the precipitous edge. With a grunt of approval, Peter again controlled his release, though it was hard not to spurt inside her slick, inviting warmth.

Hallie collapsed in a daze, unable to lift herself off of the building's edge. She mumbled incoherently in satisfaction. Peter slowly withdrew his still hard cock from her. A sly smile formed on his masculine lips. She was exactly where he wanted her to be. Her body was too weakened by pleasure to deny him anything. She was his to do with what he pleased. For this moment, he owned her.

'Peter,' she panted.

'I'm not done with you yet.'

'Give me a second, I can't move,' she begged, laughing. She closed her eyes, no longer concerned with falling over the edge. Her heart hammered in her chest.

'Good,' he said with a swarthy chuckle.

Peter massaged himself gently, enjoying the glide of her slick juices still on his penis. He stroked his hand between her legs until her pussy started to once again grow moist with cream at the attention. He flicked his finger over her sensitive nub until it stiffened with acceptance. Hallie protested weakly, unable to stand on her unsteady feet. Her high heels pressed firmly into the concrete.

He rubbed his cock over her flowing moisture, to ready himself it for penetration. Then, as he heard her moan, he slowly drew the tip of his shaft up her exposed cleft to spread her soft cheeks. With a primal growl he ignored her jolt of surprise as he narrowed in over her untried hole.

He took hold of himself and nudged at her, dipping

the tip inside the tight opening. He grunted loudly in approval. Her ass clasped firmly around him like a squeezing vice. Hallie's eyes opened in wonder at the melee of nerves that jumped in response to his forbidden entrance. She didn't expect him to actually claim her in such a taboo way.

Unable to stop him, she tried to relax as she felt him glide a little deeper to break open her second purity. Her insides jumped with the giddiness of a virgin. His cock stretched her mercilessly and Hallie gasped in a combination of wonder and gratification. Hearing her soft pants of excitement, Peter smiled victoriously and eased inside her completely. He huffed in gratification as she tensed and squeezed her canal.

With the aid of her juices he began to move within her, slowly at first and then more insistently when she could not find the words to protest. Feeling the ultimate pleasure of domination, he began to jerk within her. He felt himself losing complete control as he took her. It had been his fantasy to have the proper, conservative Hallie for so long. He wanted to control her, to take her in a way she had never been taken before. She had been his obsession.

Hallie felt a strange, warm feeling spread over her midsection. Her entire form began to tremble in fulfilment as he pounded at her tight core. And then she exploded with a tight-lipped cry of pleasure.

It was too much for Peter, who grunted and released himself inside of her with a howl, coming in hot streaming jets. When he finished, he fell against her back, completely spent, pressing Hallie into the rough stone ledge. Their sweaty skin slid together, cooling in the wind, and Peter pulled his cock from her ass with a slow groan of contentment. Hallie shivered.

Pushing up from the ledge, she turned to him. Her eyes glittered with wicked contentment. Licking her lips as she righted her clothing, she watched him button his fly. When he looked at her it was from under lowered lashes.

'I am sure going to miss you,' Peter said with a lopsided grin. His devilishly black hair fell over his eyes.

'Miss me?' she questioned in alarm. 'Are you firing me?'

'Your promotion came through this morning. You leave for Paris in two weeks.' Peter hummed contentedly as he turned from her. With a smirk, he threw over his shoulder, 'Oh, and you're definitely getting a raise.' He pulled the roof key from his front pocket.

She watched his naked back draw farther away from her. Whistling, he unlocked the thick metal door and disappeared within the dark passageway. The door shut loudly behind him and then all was silent.

Turning back to the ledge, Hallie sighed. A smile came to her lips as she revelled in the rapture of her sated body.

'Goodbye, Peter,' she said, 'I'll miss you, too. Even though I barely got to know you.'

Michelle M Pillow is the author of the Cheek titles *Fierce Competition*, *Opposites Attract* and *Bit by the Bug*. Her novel, *Along for the Ride*, is published by Cheek in August 2007.

The Apprentice Fiona Locke

Master Leighton was right. His apprentice played flawlessly after a caning.

Three sharp strokes to the seat of the lad's trousers. No ceremony. Just swift correction for a sour note. And Martin played the piece again. Perfectly.

'Excellent,' said Master Leighton. It was the only time he ever used the word, the only time he ever sounded truly pleased. He wasn't so much praising his apprentice as praising himself for eliciting the impeccable recital.

It was a hard life with Master Leighton, but well worth it. He was the most brilliant violinist in the country and he was extremely selective about his pupils. Strict discipline was a condition of his tutelage, a condition that discouraged many less dedicated boys from studying with him. Martin was different.

Alison twisted round in front of the mirror to see her smarting backside. The trousers offered little protection from the sting of the cane. But she was grateful for every stroke. Because she was his apprentice. And Master Leighton did not accept female pupils.

She was eighteen, but her slight build allowed her to pass for a much younger boy. It was no sacrifice to conceal her femininity. Music was her life and anything she had to surrender to pursue it was worth losing. The fact that Master Leighton wouldn't teach girls hadn't dimmed her spirits for a moment. She had simply cropped her hair, borrowed some clothes from her brother and gone to audition for him. That had been eight months ago.

It was difficult in the beginning. Alison worried that he would see through her disguise and send her away in disgrace for trying to deceive him. She fretted about how to walk, how to talk and act like a boy. But with some coaching from her brother she grew confident.

Master Leighton caned his new apprentice on the very first day, ostensibly for some careless error. Alison suspected it was more to establish his authority. She tried to take the punishment bravely, reminding herself with each stroke that she was a boy and boys didn't cry. The caning was painful, but it did not expose her ruse.

Now she no longer had to remind herself not to whimper or cry. Her boyish manners were second nature to her and she accepted her master's correction with the fortitude of any lad.

Alison gently rubbed the vivid tramlines. To her they were badges of honour. They meant she was studying with the genius.

'You're not sawing a tree limb, boy!' Master Leighton would snap, rapping Martin's knuckles sharply with his bow.

He could be tyrannical, forcing his apprentice to practise for hours on end, hammering away at a troublesome musical phrase until it was played to perfection. Eccentric and unpredictable, he was easily offended even by honest mistakes on Martin's part. Indeed, he sometimes seemed capricious, as though looking for any excuse to use the cane, whether it was truly deserved or not.

The rewards were uncountable, though. And when Master Leighton performed, Alison was allowed to sit just offstage and watch, mesmerised, dreaming of the day when she would be the one the audiences flocked to see.

As she crawled into bed, wincing at her bottom's contact with the sheet, Alison pictured her master's handsome face. His features were distinguished − sharply defined and as austere as his manners. But somehow that only made him more appealing. His black looks made her tremble, but they also made her squirm with desire. She cherished his intensity. His harsh criticisms, his severe punishments. She wanted more than anything to please him, to make him proud. Trying to keep her feelings for him under control, she showed as much affection as she dared, as much as would be appropriate from a boy apprentice. But secretly she loved him. And each time he punished her she embraced the pain as proof that he loved her too.

The cane awakened strange feelings in Alison. True, it frightened her. It hurt terribly and made sitting most unwelcome. But it got her attention and it usually corrected what it was meant to. She certainly didn't enjoy it, but neither did she resent it.

Master Leighton was uncompromising. He made every stroke count and her bottom always throbbed and burnt afterwards. But when the pain began to fade to a warm glow she felt her heart swell with even more affection for the man who had inflicted it. There was a strange comfort in submitting to his discipline.

Alison snuggled down in bed, pulling the blankets up to her chin. She sighed with contentment as she replayed the caning in her mind. She had obediently assumed the position he had taught his apprentice that first day: standing three feet back from the door, bending forwards with her feet together and her hands braced on either side of the doorway, back arched and bottom presented.

Master Leighton rarely told his apprentice how many strokes he was going to administer and the suspense was both awful and heady. She clutched the architrave, her knuckles white, counting in her head and wondering if another stroke was coming.

With a deeper sigh, Alison turned onto her side, reaching behind her to savour the heat in her bottom. She had sometimes been tempted to make some minor mistake to earn punishment, but she never got up the courage. The guilty, naughty thrill of the thought was enough to make her tingle, though, and she squeezed her legs together, trying to banish the fantasies.

He must never learn the truth. It was sometimes agonising, and Alison longed to tell him who she was. She wanted to show him the proof that girls could play as well as boys. But she didn't dare raise the subject. If he should even begin to suspect . . .

Master Leighton drew his fingers along the polished surface of the violin, admiring its construction. The instrument was like a dancer. To the eye it seemed delicate and fragile, yet it had power beyond its appearance. Its graceful lines and feminine curves were deceptive, as it could only truly be mastered in the hands of a man.

Martin was like the instrument – soft, lissom, light. The boy's voice showed no sign of changing, though he was well beyond the age when it should have done. He was moody and tender-hearted. Indeed, the music often brought tears to the lad's eyes.

Master Leighton's suspicions had been growing for several weeks, but he kept returning to the one undeniable reality: the boy was a prodigy. No girl could possibly play so well.

And yet . . .

Martin's features were androgynous. He had wide brown eyes that peered out from under long lashes. His complexion was fair, with no trace of facial hair. Long, shapely fingers gripped the fingerboard of the violin and there was a feline grace in his bowing. And music easily stirred him to emotion.

One could certainly never doubt the lad's pluck under the cane. Master Leighton had reduced boys to tears before, but Martin never cried. He took his punishment and was invariably better for it. He was far more likely to become tearful over a string of haunting minor chords than over a flogging.

The master shook his head. It couldn't be true. But the more he pondered it, the more he began to see all the little clues.

It would make perfect sense, of course. He was actually surprised no one had tried it before. Martin was the best pupil he'd ever had. There had never been another so diligent, so committed, so *passionate* about music. Was it possible that was because he had more to prove?

The more he thought about it, the more certain he became. Martin was a girl. But how could he make sure? He had no intention of dismissing the apprentice. Boy or no, Martin had a gift. There was no one who could nurture and refine that gift more than

Master Leighton. And, if he was to be completely honest, he was fond of the lad. But it was time to end the charade.

As he looked through the sheet music for the next day's lesson an idea came to him. He didn't enjoy having to punish his pupils. He regarded it as a duty. But if he *was* right about Martin's secret, the idea wasn't entirely unappealing. After all, if the boy really was a girl, she certainly deserved a thrashing for deceiving him.

It surprised him that he wasn't really angry. On the contrary, he was as impressed by the girl's audacity as he was by her talent. But he intended to humble her for it.

He put away the music he had planned to use the next day. It would have challenged Martin, but not as much as what he now had in mind.

He searched through his library for the right piece, weighing Martin's talent and skill against each one. He wanted something difficult, something just beyond his apprentice's abilities. Enough to frighten and frustrate even a seasoned player.

When he found the piece he was looking for he dusted it off. It was a concerto he had underestimated himself when he was a pupil. Its complexity belied the apparent simplicity of the notes on paper. Martin – whatever her real name was – had a rigorous lesson ahead of him. Her.

'Again,' Master Leighton said harshly. 'You insult the composer when you play it like that.'

Alison stared at the music, taken aback by its intricacy. Her master had always told her that no composer exposed the amateur more than Mozart. His music demanded perfection. Nothing less would suffice.

With unsteady hands she began again. Master Leighton stopped her after three measures.

'No, no, no! Like this.' And he played the first movement himself.

Alison was always enchanted by his playing and she could easily lose herself in it. This time, however, she watched him attentively, studying his fingers and trying not to let her emotions distract her. It was impossible. Every colour and nuance filled her with longing as her master teased hidden melodies out of the concerto.

Alison marvelled that he thought his apprentice was ready for such a composition. It was more advanced than anything he'd set her before and she didn't know whether to be honoured or terrified. One thing was certain: she didn't dare tell him it was too difficult. She'd made that mistake once. It was the hardest caning he'd ever given her.

'Now play it again.'

Taking a deep breath, she obeyed, loathing the hesitance in her rendering. She couldn't help it, though. Each time she stumbled over a phrase or altered the tempo her master winced as though she was causing him pain.

'I'm sorry, sir,' she said. 'It's much harder than it looks.'

'I know that. It's not a piece that suffers show-offs.'

She gasped. 'But, sir, I'm not –'

'Are you answering me back?'

'No, sir.'

His features relaxed into an indulgent smile as he patted her shoulder. 'No, you're not a show-off,

Martin, but you do sometimes forget that you are the servant of the music and not its master.'

Alison lowered her head, embarrassed. 'Yes, sir.'

'This piece is about melody, not technical precision, though you need the one to showcase the other.'

'Yes, sir.' Bewildered, Alison stared again at the music. Sometimes, after practising for hours, the notes would swirl into meaningless black smears as though someone had spilled ink all over the pages. These notes looked like that now. How was she ever going to master them as their poor, confounded servant?

Master Leighton rose and retrieved his coat. 'I have to go into town for a little while. Practise the concerto while I'm gone. You will play it for me when I return.'

'Yes, sir.'

When he had gone Alison played it through without stopping. It sounded ghastly and dissonant with her myriad mistakes, but she forced herself to stay with it until the end. Then she started again. It was the best way to conquer her fear of it, to show it that she wasn't going to capitulate halfway through because of a wrong note. The concerto was filled with lively little *arpeggios* and tricky phrasing. She could almost believe the music didn't want her to play it. In fact, if she hadn't heard Master Leighton play it himself, she might have doubted whether it was even playable at all. A sadistic composer, was Mozart.

After forcing her way through it five times she allowed herself a small break. Nearly an hour had passed. Now that she was a little more familiar with the music she was ready to focus on it in more detail. Without her master standing over her it was tempting to skip over the easy passages and run straight to the difficult ones, learning them with more care and diligence. She resisted the urge. In his overcritical mood Master Leighton was likely to hear it in her playing and accuse her of showing off.

As she worked her way through the music she listened to the virtuoso inside her head. She could almost tune out the hash she was making with her hands and focus instead on the memory of her master's exquisite performance. Hearing him play so beautifully made her forget how strict he was, how fond of the cane. It seemed incongruous to her that such a hard taskmaster should be capable of such artistry. But the contradiction was intoxicating. His hands were soft and considered with the instrument, yet so rough with his apprentice. She couldn't help wondering how they might be with a lover. How they might feel caressing her delicate, downy limbs, enfolding her in a passionate embrace . . .

Alison shook herself out of the daydream. If Master Leighton came home and caught her staring off into space he'd make his displeasure known. And felt. With a sigh, she lifted the violin to her chin and began to play.

Her master had been gone nearly four hours and Alison was still struggling with the music. She didn't dare stop playing. It was another of his favourite tests. The violin could be heard all the way down the street, so there was no way she could take a break and simply wait until he drew near to start playing again.

At last she heard the door and she wilted with relief. Master Leighton came in, waving a hand for her to stop. 'From the beginning,' he said, taking his seat in front of her.

Too tired to be nervous any more, she started over, dreading every note. She didn't dare look up at her master; she knew she wouldn't be able to bear any expression of disdain. He allowed her to play the *allegro* straight through and she grew confident when he didn't stop her. At last she finished. She lowered the violin and bow with shaky hands, turning to him in the hope of finding approval in his features.

Instead, he looked at her inscrutably. 'Have you *been* practising?' he asked. 'Or just staring at the music?'

Alison's mouth fell open. 'I haven't stopped playing since you left, sir,' she said, baffled.

'Then perhaps you need another four hours.'

She stared at him in disbelief, not knowing what to say. Couldn't he see that she'd been working hard? Couldn't he *hear*? 'It's a difficult piece, sir,' she said weakly. 'I just need more time.'

'Then you shall have it.' Master Leighton rose from his seat, deliberately. 'I'm going back out. While I'm away you will learn this piece. You will practise until I return and I don't care if your fingers fall off, boy. Then I expect to hear you play it properly.' He left the threat unspoken.

Alison hung her head. 'Yes, sir.'

'I can only think your mind is somewhere other than on your studies.'

Miserable, Alison assured him that she was as dedicated as he could hope.

'We'll see about that,' he replied. And with that, he left again.

Alison blinked back her tears and looked at the clock. It was nearly two and she hadn't eaten. Her stomach was complaining and her hands would begin to shake if she didn't eat something.

'No,' she told herself disgustedly. If something as trivial as hunger could distract her, then she wasn't focused enough. She'd actually known her master to *forget* to eat. And it was only when she suggested it to him that he realised he was hungry at all.

Armed with fierce determination to prove herself to Master Leighton, the apprentice took a deep breath and began the concerto again.

It was another four hours before Alison allowed herself a break. She was exhausted. Her neck was stiff and her wrists and fingers ached in a way they hadn't since her first gruelling day of apprenticeship. She had a permanent bruise from the chin rest, but the unremitting practice had deepened it so that the slightest pressure was agony. She couldn't believe the violin strings hadn't cut through her fingers. The deep grooves burnt and tingled from the pressure of the fingerboard. But for all that, she'd forgotten her hunger.

She was beginning to wonder if her master would ever return. She went to the window and peered down the street. There was no sign of him.

A sudden, terrible thought seized her like an intruder's hand. What if something had happened to him? Tears sprang to her eyes at once and she swallowed her panic, trying to calm herself. It wasn't unusual for him to disappear for hours at a time. No doubt he needed his space from her. She didn't suppose that the company of his apprentice was as captivating as that of his acquaintances in town.

Or lady friends.

The image was unbidden and unwelcome, but once seen, it couldn't be unseen. It had never occurred to her before. She had always taken it for granted that he was too consumed with music to have time for a relationship. But now Alison was forced to confront the possibility. Was he off amusing himself with some exotic creature while his poor apprentice slaved away in his absence?

Alison tried to resume her practice, but the feelings wouldn't dissipate. She couldn't banish the thought of her master in the arms of an alluring paramour, laughing and enjoying her stimulating company. Her playing suffered for the preoccupation. Frustrated tears were beginning to sting her eyes when she finally heard the door.

At first she didn't know whether she was relieved that he was unharmed or angry that he'd deigned to return from his tryst. She looked up at him, weary and confused. He didn't notice.

'All right, let's hear it, lad,' he said without pre-amble. He sat in front of her and crossed his arms expectantly.

Alison couldn't read anything in his tone or his expression to tell her if her suspicions were true. Resentfully, she played the *allegro* for him. In her own eyes her performance had all the colour and passion of dishwater, though she hadn't missed a single note. A hollow victory, she thought bitterly.

Master Leighton stared at her for a long time, his brow furrowed, as though trying to puzzle out the change in his apprentice. He seemed to be searching for something to say.

'I didn't miss a note, sir,' Alison supplied, making no attempt to disguise her bitterness.

Her provocative tone made his eyes flash and he straightened in his chair. 'Indeed you didn't,' he agreed. 'But I doubt if that would have impressed Mozart.'

Alison lifted her chin a little at this slight. She ground her teeth to keep from responding in kind. She was frightened by the intensity of her feelings. She knew better than to cross swords with him, but she feared things were about to come to a head.

'You will therefore play it again,' he continued. 'And you will keep playing it until I'm satisfied. You will not be dismissed until then. Do you understand? My master set me this piece when I was your age and I had to play it over and over until I got it right.'

It was too much. All the confused emotions that had been simmering below the surface erupted in a flash of fury. 'Your master was as much of a sadist as you are, then!' she snarled, lashing out at the music stand with her foot. It fell with a clatter on the floor, scattering the sheet music. The pages fluttered around them and drifted to the floor with a loud papery flapping as Alison realised what she'd done.

Master Leighton was staring at her and she thought there was something triumphant in his eyes.

Several seconds passed in excruciating silence while she watched him, terrified.

At last he spoke. 'Right.' It was just one word, but the cold and precise way he enunciated it made her shudder.

Now she was for it. He'd once given his apprentice a dozen strokes just for questioning him; this outburst had to be worth three times that.

'Fetch the cane.'

It was amazing, the way those simple words could make her regret so much. The stress of the demanding practice had made her reckless and insolent. And jealous. Who was she to question her master or make assumptions about him?

Hanging her head in shame, she brought him the cane as she'd done so many times before. He nodded towards the door and she went there, her feet dragging.

'I've clearly been too lenient with you,' said Master Leighton. 'I've allowed you the protection of your trousers whenever I've caned you. But in showing me such blatant disrespect you've lost that privilege. Take them off.'

Alison's eyes were wide with horror. Oh, what had she done? If he caned her without her trousers he'd uncover her deception. Then he would turn her out.

'I'm waiting.'

Alison had no choice but to do as he said, silently praying that he would let her leave her underpants on. Their scant cover would offer no protection from the cane, but they would keep her secret. Perhaps Master Leighton wouldn't notice anything amiss.

With great reluctance, she unfastened her trousers and pulled them down, slipping them off. The air in the room was hot and dusty; nonetheless, it chilled her as it touched her bare legs. She felt more exposed than she ever had before. Blinking back tears, she leant forwards to take hold of the door frame, pressing her legs tightly together.

She heard his step on the wooden floor behind her and she gritted her teeth, expecting the first stroke. Instead, she felt his fingers in the waistband of her underpants. Before she could draw a breath to protest, he had yanked them down to her ankles.

Alison froze. She waited for him to denounce her. Instead, she heard the low whistle of the cane as he sliced it through the air in preparation, making her jump. He hadn't seen anything.

Mustering all her willpower, Alison locked her legs and rooted her feet tightly to the floor. Maybe if she was perfectly still, if she didn't twist or squirm too much . . .

Master Leighton was behind her. 'Now then,' he said. 'Let's see if we can teach you some respect.'

Alison had never felt the cane on her bare skin before and she flinched at the cold length of it against her flesh. She uttered a little squeak, but kept her knees and ankles pressed together as tightly as she could. The cane tapped gently, each tap getting harder and harder, leading up to the first stroke. Her master didn't usually draw it out like this. He believed in summary punishment with no frills. But she had really angered him this time.

She held her breath as the cane drew back and struck her with a meaty smack. Hard. She gasped, but stayed in position as the pain began to flower in a savage line across her bottom. She never thought her trousers afforded her much protection, but feeling the cane without them as a barrier, she realised just how wrong she'd been.

Again the cane rose and fell, cleaving the air and then her backside. Alison hissed through her teeth, but focused all her energy on preserving her secret. If she could survive this, she'd never give him cause to cane her again. Then he would never know she was really a girl.

The caning grew more intense with each stroke and, while she managed to keep her legs straight and together, she was unable to keep from crying out.

That wouldn't give her away, though; any boy would yelp from such a caning.

When Master Leighton stopped she released the breath she'd been holding. He occasionally paused in the middle of a severe caning. She never knew whether it was over or whether he was deciding how much more she deserved. This time she didn't dare to hope that he would stop there.

He stood directly behind her, inspecting the damage. She heard the creak of the floorboards as he crouched down to look more closely.

Suddenly, there was the cool touch of his finger as he traced the weals left by the cane. Alison shuddered. She could feel his breath on the backs of her legs.

'Mm-hmm,' was his only response.

He stood up again.

'You know what comes next, boy,' he said. 'Feet apart.'

This was a command she'd always dreaded, even with her trousers on, because of the way it tautened the fabric across her backside and opened up new areas for the attack of the cane. Now she dreaded it for an entirely different reason. She opened her mouth and turned her head to plead with him, but he cut her off.

'Feet apart.'

Well, this was it. He would see now. She inched her feet apart and waited for him to discover the truth.

Instead, the cane sliced into her again. And again. And again. He didn't allow much time between the strokes and she barely had time to recover from one before the next fell. Each one hurt terribly, but the torment of knowing that any second he would learn the truth was far worse than the pain.

'Wider,' he said gruffly.

The inevitability was agony. How could he not see? Could he possibly be so focused on her bottom that he just didn't notice? As a girl Alison was very pretty. And unclothed, it was inconceivable that he couldn't tell. Her plump bottom, shapely legs and girlish figure should have been apparent long before now, not to mention the obvious. But no. The cane continued to do its worst while she yelped and cried under it.

She had lost count of the strokes. It was well over a dozen, possibly even two. She was dazed. As much by confusion as by pain. So dazed, in fact, that she didn't even realise when he stopped.

Master Leighton was silent for a long time.

Alison's heart sank. It was over. He'd seen. Tears streamed down her face. She refused to make a sound, though. She wouldn't disgrace herself any further with hiccupping, childish sobs.

She clung to the architrave as though letting go of it would also mean letting go of her dignity. The punishment was over. The charade was over. Her life was over. She couldn't move.

The floorboards creaked and she trembled. He was inspecting her again. Not the marks this time, but her sex. No doubt he was shaking his head in disgust over her folly. Reassuring himself that he was right about the inferiority of female musicians. The feeling of exposure was hard to endure, but she dared not move until he instructed her to.

But instead of cursing her and ordering her out, he traced the lines of the cane again. Slowly. Thoroughly. As though savouring each one. Alison shivered in spite of herself. So many times she had wanted him to touch her like this. Now it was to be the first and the last time.

But there was something odd about the familiarity in his touch. It was soothing and gentle. Not the touch of a master examining his punished pupil at all. It was the touch of a lover. The finger trailed over her burning flesh, coming to rest in the centre, near her bottom crease. Then, one by one the pads of the other fingers descended until his entire palm rested lightly on her bottom.

Alison was afraid to breathe. One breath could disrupt the stillness she never wanted to end.

The hand patted her and then continued down to the cleft between her cheeks.

She closed her eyes.

Then the hand cupped her firmly between the legs and gave a little squeeze.

A jolt surged through her at his touch.

The hand between her legs told her more than words ever could. She gripped the doorway, arching her back into the sensation. Her legs felt as though they would give way beneath her. The warmth in her bottom spread through her body, unfolding like scrolls.

Her master softly smacked the insides of her thighs with his fingertips, urging her legs further apart.

Blushing, Alison obeyed, painfully aware of the dampness between them.

He stroked her softness, drawing his fingers across the little slit as though teasing music from it with his bow. He smoothed the moist folds and drew closer to her.

He took away his hand and she tensed. Then she

felt his own arousal as he pressed himself against her sore bottom.

Her knees threatened to buckle and he took hold of her wrists and prised her from the doorway. She sank into his arms and he turned her around to face him. She couldn't meet his eyes. He didn't force her to. With a sigh she let herself go as he unbuttoned and unlaced her boy's clothes and led her to his room. He guided her to the bed and she sat down, wincing at the freshly awakened discomfort in her bottom.

Master Leighton smiled. He pushed her down on her back and she looked up at him for the first time since the caning. In place of his usual temperamental scowl there was a tender expression she had never seen before.

Then he kissed her, pressing his mouth into hers with firm, gentle force. He cupped her small breasts, squeezing them gently, tweaking her nipples until they stiffened.

Her body surrendered as his hands explored her, acquainting him with her femininity. She wrapped her legs around him, urging him closer, tighter. He moulded her curves to his angles as he took possession, driving himself deeply into her wetness. The roughness of the bed beneath her punished flesh wrenched a muffled yelp from her. But she absorbed the rising notes of pain, grinding her hips into him greedily. Her mentor, her master.

She was unprepared for the sudden spasms of pleasure that consumed her, overlapping like the notes of a swirling symphony. He clutched her tightly, urgently, as he filled her with the hot jets of his own climax.

Satiated and spent, she panted for breath, her head resounding with the music of release.

After a languorous, breathless silence he smoothed a damp lock of hair away from her forehead and kissed her there. He was smiling. 'What's your name?' he asked.

She flushed. 'Alison, sir.'

He repeated the name, as though tasting a new wine. 'Alison. You are as lovely as your playing.'

They were words the long-suffering apprentice had never dreamt she would hear from him. Tears shone in her eyes. 'Thank you, sir,' she whispered.

He chuckled. 'I don't think it's necessary for you to call me "sir" any longer.'

Alison turned on her side and reached back to touch her tender bottom, to reawaken the sting. The pleasure was so much sweeter for the harmony with pain. 'I know,' she said. 'Sir.'

Fiona Locke's short stories have appeared in numerous Wicked Words collections. Her first novel, *Over the Knee*, is published by Nexus Enthusiast.